JAY STURNER

# THE HUNCHBACK'S CAPTIVE

### and Others

STORIES AND POEMS

OF THE DARKLY FANTASTIC

D0291666

Fairy Thrush Press

*To Kelly and Garion*

# THE HUNCHBACK'S CAPTIVE

## AND OTHERS

# Table of Contents

# Sketch by Sketch

*Inspired by "The Kith of the Elf Folk" by Lord Dunsany*

These I have drawn: a hillside of moonlit clover; creeks cradled by heather; a forest beyond the stone walls of a pasture. And all just to get home; I've been gone so very long.

Today you'll find me in the green layers beyond the city, sidestepping the coiled corpses of men's dreams, bypassing industrial towns where mechanical beasts gnaw on adolescent hearts. For out here dwell the kith of my childhood: the salamander, fox, rook, and deer. Old friends too are the mosses and ferns, the spirits of pollen, the ghosts of tree rings. All under the watchful eye of Pan.

You see, my troubles began as a child. I had become obsessed with humans, would sketch their tall bodies and lively faces on everything from peeled birch bark to rain puddles to hardened flows of sap. I read and reread all the stories about them— romantic tales of knights and beautiful maidens, of epic battles and hidden treasures. To me, the human soul mirrored endless romance and wonder. The mortals, it seemed, dared to dream of anything—they dared to dream of *us*.

O how I longed to dance and love and sketch wildly among them! To escape the confines of Pan's wild domain—to posses a soul!

1

Such desires led to secrecy, to a thousand sketches wrought in the abandoned swamps where not even the banshee would go. Over time, and at the pace of a snail's whisper, the leaves of my face turned autumn and blew away. My wings shriveled and fell. I had somehow willed myself, sketch by sketch, into the abrasive, mortal light of Man.

Alas, the humans were not at all as I had expected. Romance played almost no role in courtship or marriage. Foreign to me was their hunger, pain, deep sadness. Strange and worrisome were science and religion. Hardships overcame me, and I soon found myself bowing to the snickering god of apathy. Before long my eyes turned the colour of winter, and my mind broke apart as a flower in a storm. I do not know if I ever gained a soul.

Yet despite my disappointments, one small comfort always remained: my ability to sketch, though I no longer draw anything related to mortals or their dead dreams. Instead I lose myself in the mossy wood and wild heath, desperate to reveal the true music and landscapes of my youth. Always I am trying my best to get the details just right. It is all I can do to return, for I am at the mercy of human imagination.

# Faerystruck Down

In the rolling fog of the purple sea
Where slugs infest the ridge
    And breeze-bent heather
    Tethers ghosts of the drowned

Beyond the threshold of the mind
Where sea hags howl at the moon
    And shapes unseen
    Sneak away human babes

Lies the maritime trail I was warned not walk
Urged by patrons of the old pub
To return to America, and be gone at next breath:
    "For too tempting is the tourist from afar!"

But I split my sides at their heathen pleas
Doused their cares with whiskey and ale
Till after a spell, I was cheered out of town
    Pushed along streets of leaping whispers

So onward to accursed shores I went
Bold with humor and the prod of drink
    Where fish-lipped merrows in *cohuleen druiths*
    Leered from frothy kelp isles

And the mutterings in belch-bogs grew ever near . . .
And the perverted, creeping shadows . . .

I will never forget their dream-drenched faces
As they sang and danced and picked over my end
Goblets high in the salty spray of the purple sea
Where many a mortal bone now rests in the deep

And in my last moments of earthly acquaintance,
Head a pivot and lit with fires green,
They branded my soul to the tongue of lore
Forever to break out madly from seaside lips

# What We Know of Goddesses

*for W.H. Pugmire*

Atop great mountains, on high thrones, sit the gods—beards long and glowing with the light of dead stars. Always their dark, playful eyes are hot with mischief. They delight in a belief that the goddesses are impressed by their whimsical creations, amused even. Surely they got a kick out of *Homo sapiens*, that inferior clay fumbling wildly over the layout of design—such fodder for comedy! Perhaps. But in dull pockets of timelessness, when the bearded ones are idle, the goddesses—because it is their way—have been known to nurture humanity's fetal spirit, to channel love there, to plant seeds of art and philosophy, to spark ambition, and curiosity. Myriad tasks are assigned to fairies, mystics, and angels; demons too, if they should lead to a truth. Much then becomes enhanced in the spectra of human souls, in the course of man's future. Sure, the gods are ingenious and powerful in their ways; of that there is no doubt. But lest they forget, they are equaled. Very much equaled.

# Strings

A young man in shabby clothing drops off a dark, windswept cliff. Flashbacks tear through his mind: a catching glimpse of Kate's eyes at the marionette show; their first kiss on the beach; her handkerchief waving him off to Europe; the final, pleading letter he failed to answer. Other flashbacks reveal clues to his despair: dead comrades in smoking battlefields; the long, painful hospital stay; sleepless nights beneath bridges; a thief scampering off with his puppet case.

*Kate sleeps soundly in her lighthouse across the sea, the moon full and bright over the Maine landscape. A wooden marionette sits on a nearby chair, a figure sculpted by Martin in his own image; a gift in his time away. It leans forward, slow and deliberate, like a plant leaning toward the sun.*

Waves crash and spray against Martin's inert body. He slides off the barnacled rocks on a layer of blood, slips into the cold ocean and floats facedown beneath indifferent stars. Salt water fills his lungs. He sinks into darkness.

*The marionette slides off the chair to the moonlit floor. Kate moans, turns to her side, dark hair falling across the shoulder of her white nightgown. In a dream, a handsome puppeteer waves from a transport ship and disappears into the fog.*

Tiny fish dart about the darkness, nipping at Martin's skin. He feels no pain, yet there's an awareness of submergence, of a heaviness thrust against his body and limbs. He lingers in a cloud of blood, waiting for the nightmare to end, to be released from limbo into God's arms.

*Wobbling on skinny legs, the marionette gets to its feet and lurches forward, dragging its cross-handle. It falls to its knees several times as if under a great weight. "Martin, is that you?" Kate whispers.*

A jellyfish flits through the blackness. It is strikingly beautiful, illuminating the dark like a green moon in a turbid sky. Kate's face coruscates inside of it, piercing Martin's soul, tempting him to embrace her. But his body is useless, he cannot move. So his thoughts turn to puppetry, to the manipulation of inanimate objects: strings are envisioned on his arms, legs, shoulders, and head, all controlled by a higher force. This he imagines. And when thick, tangible strings actually *do* appear, seemingly from nowhere, it fills his heart with hope, triggering a telekinetic response that plucks and dances his body toward the passing eidolon.

*The marionette now moves steadily toward Kate's bed, the cross-handle lifting it into the air. Wooden legs clank together as it floats to a bedpost and wraps its segmented arms around the ornate finial. Kate rises, grabs a green bottle off the nightstand, and clambers barefoot out the window between billowing curtains. Outside, she sleepwalks beneath the rotating lighthouse beam. The puppet lands in the grass behind her and begins to follow.*

Strings twist and tangle chaotically around Martin's distended body in their haste to pull him toward the jellyfish. But there is no need for the grace of a stage performance here. If he can simply catch the elusive jellyfish and wrap his arms around it—wrap his arms around *her*—then he and Kate will enter a new world together; of that he is certain—the appearance of the strings a sign of divine guidance. And the closer he gets to the apparition, the clearer her face within that ghostly green glow.

*Kate meanders down a moonlit path of sand, rock, and stunted pine, bottle clutched tight against her chest. The puppet jerks its way along a few feet behind, elevated cross-handle twisting from side to side as if gripped by an invisible hand. She traverses a swath of windblown grass and arrives at a steep ledge over the crashing sea. There she pauses, leans forward, sways. The marionette creeps up behind her.*

Martin is now moving at a tremendous speed. Water rushes into his mouth, nose, and ears like wet cement. The writhing bodies of myriad creatures press up and quiver against his blue flesh, causing him to lose sight of Kate. But he knows the strings will guide him right, that their sole purpose is to reunite him with his lost love.

*Rolled up inside the bottle is the most difficult letter Kate has ever had to write: a letter which speaks of terrible waiting, of the sadness of saying goodbye, of the heart's need to move on. She casts it to the waves as the wind blows wildly through her hair. The marionette wobbles up beside her and peers down at the floating bottle. Now its legs twist; the knees buckle. The puppet drops from the edge and falls to the barnacled rocks below; a moment later it slides into the foam.*

The strings lift Martin out of the sea and into the cold, starry night. Water spills away in a white rush. With a wet thud he is flung across the deck of a ship where he rolls and flops in a landslide of sea things; a slimy mass of scales and fins and tiny mouths gasping for air, the jellyfish not among them.

*Kate returns to the nearby swath of grass and lies down. The lighthouse beam circles quietly overhead. She shuts her eyes in peaceful repose, lets new, unanchored dreams rise to the surface. Meanwhile, the marionette floats out to sea, its face covered in moonlight, one arm slung over the glimmering green bottle. Across the ocean, a fishing vessel sounds its horn, heads to port.*

# The Girl with the Crooked Spine

Her skin is like leather. What remains of her reddish hair sits in a tuft beside her mummified head. She has no arms or legs, though both feet and her right hand lay alongside her torso. The eyes deteriorated almost two thousand years ago, long before her well-preserved body was dug out of the peat near Yde, a village in the Netherlands, and placed in this traveling exhibit. She was sixteen years old the day she died, and her spine, like Patrick's, was horribly twisted by scoliosis.

Archaeologists call her Yde Girl. Patrick calls her Edie.

Propped up beside the display case is a poster of the girl's suggested appearance. Using a wax-head reconstruction, the image depicts a teenage girl with wavy reddish hair, a high forehead, and what some might consider an intelligent but sad countenance. The exhibit, titled 'Bog Bodies of Europe,' also includes Lindow Man, Tollund Man, and the Girl of the Uchter Moor, among others, each fragmented body displayed in small, personalized exhibit rooms adjoined by dim corridors.

\*　\*　\*

It's a late Sunday afternoon in January. Snow accumulates outside the Field Museum in Chicago, long drifts rising across the steps of the main entrance. In the distance, Snowy Owls, on winter leave from Canada, sit on elongated water breaks, their sleepy, golden eyes scanning for ducks on the gray surface of Lake Michigan. Few cars populate the streets, and despite the storm, Patrick has come to see Edie. It's his seventh visit.

As he enters the exhibit, Patrick wiggles out of his backpack and lets it slide down his left arm, the side of him that is slightly higher than his right. He pauses to admire the photo of Edie's reconstructed face, the version of her he prefers—though he does address the fragmented body now and then, so as to not seem disrespectful.

"Hello Edie," Patrick says, pushing aside his red bangs. He reaches into his backpack for a spiral notebook. "Big storm out there today. We almost didn't come, but I told my mom I had a paper due tomorrow." He laughs. "She's so gullible sometimes! Anyway, we took the bus and it was totally fine. She's over in the gift shop right now."

Though Edie's hardships had undoubtedly been more profound than his own, Patrick could still identify with how he imagined she must have felt all those years ago. Surely she had been stared at, pointed at, laughed at—all by superstitious people that did not, or would not, understand her deformity. And this deformity had probably led to her death, as it was theorized that she had been beaten, choked, and stabbed in a sacrifice to the gods.

Now, roughly two thousand years later, her naked remains lay exposed in wizened, leathery fragments atop a sterile white slab—a static, lonely darkness curled tight about her display case. Worst of all is the frayed rope, an instrument of her death, still wrapped loosely about her neck.

"You should've seen it, Edie," Patrick says, inching closer to the photo. "There's this *gorgeous* Cecropia Moth in the entomology exhibit. It's huge!" He shifts his torso to the right in an attempt to gain comfort in his back brace. "In fact, they're the largest silk moths in North America. At night, in summer, you can sometimes find them near artificial lights."

Realizing she may not understand "artificial lights," Patrick gestures to the track lighting over her display case.

"Most people aren't even aware that these beautiful creatures exist," he adds. "Kinda sad, actually." His eyes follow a swirl pattern on the floor as he grows lost in thought.

"Before he died," he continues, still looking at the floor, "my dad used to show me all the best places to find them. That's when I really got interested in nature and stuff." He shakes his head. "I don't know. I keep trying to get my mom to go out and look for them with me, but besides butterflies, she pretty much hates insects. She thinks they're all going to bite her. Anyway, my friend José, he used to help me catch them all the time. That was awhile ago though, before he got hooked on video games and stuff, so . . . I usually just go out by myself now."

Edie lies silent in her display case. All is quiet but for the subdued howling of the wind over the museum.

By his third visit, Patrick had come to believe that Edie's presence lingered within her small exhibit room, a presence that grew stronger—more intimate, it seemed—with each of his visits. And today, perhaps because the museum is virtually empty, he welcomes the feeling that her spirit has leaned up against his crooked body and under his arm for comfort, the snowstorm blowing forcefully across the high roof. In such an atmosphere, mixed with the quietude of the museum's closing hour, Patrick imagines he can hear her breathing beneath the persistent drone of the heating vents, occasionally feeling a slight flinch from her asymmetrical shoulders when a far-off door slams or a noisy child disturbs the tranquility. Her hair gives off the scent of heather, and this conjures up the image of a lush, boundless moor.

"I . . . I wrote you something," Patrick says, opening his notebook. He flips to the desired page, freckled face turning a light shade of red. "It's sort of a—well, it's like a poem."

To keep from being heard outside the thin, temporary walls of the exhibit, Patrick lowers his voice: *I call it 'To a Girl from Yde'.*"

Edie's display lights flicker, their low, electric hum filling the tight space of the exhibit. The eyes in the photo stare ahead while shadows pulsate across the walls, stretching and retracting as the lights continue to flicker. Patrick twists his torso, pressing a free hand over his back brace for stability, then continues.

*"I am here, as a friend*
*A kindred soul of tomorrow*
*To offer my heart*
*To a girl who knew much sorrow"*

The storm howls and whips across the sky. And though the massive building seems impenetrable, a rogue wind finds its way in and wanders sharply down the marbled, columned halls. Floor by floor it brushes against glass cases and interpretive signs of myriad exhibits, past the Charles Knight murals, in and out of the gift shop and café, through the angry skull of Sue, the T. rex.

"Oh my gawd, Brian, this one is *really* gross!" A woman in her early twenties, holding hands with a guy who looks visibly exhausted by the museum, comes bounding into Yde Girl's exhibit from the corridor. Patrick back steps into the outlying darkness. With her phone the woman snaps a few quick, thoughtless photos of the bog body and the couple giggles their way out.

"I'm *so* sick of people like that," Patrick says. "Stupid, self-centered jerks—I *hate* them!" He sighs, shaking his head as he eases back into the light of the display case. He stares into a corner, lost in thought, then turns to Edie's photo.

"I'm sorry," he says, pushing aside his bangs. "I just, I just get so *mad* sometimes. I mean, why do they say things like that? It's beyond rude!" He regards Edie's fragmented remains. "You know what? I couldn't care less if I *ever* saw another human being again for as long as I live. Seriously. There isn't anyone else besides you that—" He turns away, embarrassed. "Forget it. You're probably sick of me by now anyway. I'll just . . . I'll just finish this stupid poem and go."

Dust falls from the edge of the display case; a large mote floats off into the darkness. Sighing, he continues with the poem.

*"I give you these words*
*That arose from our meeting*
*To help end the loneliness*
*That the both of us are feeling—"*

An announcement comes over the loudspeaker, indicating that the museum will be closing in ten minutes.

"Patrick, the museum's going to close in ten minutes." It's Patrick's mother. She's sticking her head into the exhibit.

"I know, mom. Everyone hears that announcement. I'll be out in a minute."

"Just letting you know. We need to get going or we'll miss the next bus."

Her head retreats into the corridor, and Patrick listens to her footsteps as they move along the walls of the exhibit, going a short distance until they reach a nearby bench. He hears her sit down and rummage through her purse.

"*Jeez*," Patrick says, rolling his eyes with a slight grin. In the photo, Yde Girl stares off to Patrick's left. The eye sockets of her partially collapsed head are set directly on him.

He continues with the poem, a bit unsteady on his feet.

*"Let's break the barrier—"*

He pauses, grimacing in pain from having stood too long in one spot. He decides to support the bulk of his weight against the display case as he recites the final lines of the poem.

*"Let's break the barrier*
*And walk hand in hand*
*Across all time & space*
*To the moors of our own land"*

A security guard approaches the exhibit as he goes about his route.

"My son's in there," Patrick's mother says, pointing with one hand and snapping shut her compact with the other. "He's taking notes for a school paper. He'll be out in just a minute." She smiles at the man, who responds with a lazy yawn. Outside, the blizzard presses up against the museum.

*Pop!*—Broken glass hits the floor.

The guard spins on his heel, rips a flashlight from his belt and scrambles into the exhibit. Patrick's mother chases after him. There, a low fog drifts down the shattered display case and rolls between their legs, the stench of rotten peat permeating the air.

As the fog clears they see Patrick's back brace wobble to a stop on Yde Girl's remains.

The boy's mother screams. The security guard throws a meaty arm across her lunging body, yells into his radio. Stumbling back, she shouts her son's name from the wall as the guard frantically shines his flashlight into each corner of the room.

No further trace of Patrick was ever found.

# Misery of He Who is Outside the Realm of Man

He who is outside the realm of man suffers a deep, unrelenting misery. Left, for reasons known only to the gods, to ponder his existence within the cosmic fog outside space and time. To know only his purpose, his destiny, a task performed mindlessly and without pause.

As a consequence, many questions relative to his plight arise but are never answered. He bears no recollection of birth, no sense of an earlier time or even of time itself, save for hints gleaned from the collective awareness of mankind as it fumbles through its existence.

He is unable to interact with humans. Yet now and again come flashes of once having *been* human: a spear stuck into a dying mammoth, the eyes of a woman and child, his hand painting horses on a cave wall . . . and then, the sudden visitation of the gods.

Adding to his misery is the probability that these flashes are merely residual energies from the endless stream of souls passing through his bony fingers. Fingers that once painted, or so it seems.

*Was I truly once a man?* he wonders. *And if so, how long must I endure this lonely, miserable state? How long before I may again know the*

15

*excitement of a hunt, the touch of a woman, the thrill of creating? Certainly there is another to replace me.*

He cannot help but be convinced of a return to life, for all souls make their way back to Earth in one form or another—to this cycle he is witness.

But he who is outside the realm of man, and whose core is a diamond of misery, must endure his current destiny without fail, for always there is war and disease, starvation, murder, agedness . . . .

For who knew, that he who had first painted the wonders of life had angered the gods. That with a cave wall and crude ochres had brought forth an appreciation of art and beauty, thus giving man a proper soul.

And so, for his role in revealing those deeper layers, for strengthening humanity beyond the gods' intentions, the first painter of life was made a lonely gatekeeper of death. Forever to guide the very souls he helped create.

# Time to Grow Up Where There's No Time at All

You simply do not exist, they assert with buttoned-up stares,
Though I've detected salty scents on the curled tongues of butterflies,
And feet-shapes where the grass and clover straighten their necks.
Get your head out of the mist, they keep telling me,
There are no such beasts in the world.
But I think I saw you once, at the corner of my eye.
Yes, I truly believe I did! For you were tall and fleshy and sad,
Just like the drawings in my secret book of lore: Its spider silk pages
Guiding my dreams beyond the moonlight.

# Belch

The planet hasn't been this warm for millions of years. Jungle is the new skin. A spinous beast of flesh-and-stone comes along and gnaws on the dying cities, swallows all it can manage. It meanders along the blossoming curve of earth, coughing up guns and concrete, art and cell phones, machinery and bones. Now it bays at the indifferent moon, its belly fat with the lingering screams of monochrome souls. Its gut swells, heaves, rumbles like an angry volcano. And before curling down for another million-year nap, it drops its forest-covered jaw and lets out a putrid, roaring belch—expelling the failed god of a thing called Man.

# Charon Falls into the Styx

A skinny old man stands on the shore of the river Styx. He removes his tie and suit jacket. Next his dress shoes, slacks, and pressed shirt. He always hated being dressed like that, even as a funeral director. Why didn't his wife bury him in his Hawaiian shirt like he'd asked? She never did listen, that woman.

Charon emerges from the fog in his creaky wooden boat. Seeing the old man in nothing but black socks and tighty-whities causes him to snicker. This leads to heavy laughter, which in turn leads to a hoarse guffaw. In fact, he laughs so hard he loses his balance and tumbles forward off the boat and into the river. Seeing this, the old man scowls. That is not very professional, he thinks. I could do a *much* better job than that fool!

Charon clambers back into the boat and reaches for his pole, still laughing. He squeezes the water from his shroud and pulls the hood up over his pale dome. As the boat nears the shore he motions for the nearly-naked man to step aboard. The old-timer climbs in and glares at the ferryman. Neither speaks.

Finally, Charon holds out an upturned hand. "Um, got my fee?" he asks with a slight chuckle. "Maybe in that . . . spiffy jacket on shore there?" He looks away while biting his tongue to keep from laughing. The old man sighs heavily, digs into the front of his underwear, and pulls out a gold coin. A curly gray hair falls into the boat as he offers the payment to Charon, who takes a step back. "No, keep it! Keep it!" he laughs, dropping the pole to grab his heaving sides. "Please!"

And once again Charon falls off his boat and into the river Styx—only this time he disappears beneath the waves. When the shroud resurfaces, the geezer bends down and pulls it aboard, then wraps it over his proud shoulders. Flesh drops off his bones as cries of suffering arise in the distance. Throwing up his hood, the old man grabs the pole and pushes off into the fog.

# The Hunchback's Captive

I was facedown in swamp muck beneath a moss green moon, gasping for air and choking on aquatic slimes, when a female hunchback grabbed me by the ankles and pulled me ashore. Red will-o'-the-wisps twirled through the fog about us while dark pines creaked ominously overhead.

What had led me to sleepwalk to such a place? Had I been dreaming of what might lay beyond the edge of the city, far from its apathetic citizenry, tangible greed, all that privilege and expectation? Away from the howls and squeals of cars, trains, and other oiled machines? Had my soul looked to escape the leech-suck of it all?

And who was this savior of mine, this decrepit hag wearing nothing but a potato sack for a garment? I inquired, but she would not speak. Instead she hummed, though not in any musical sense. Rather, that soft buzzing deep within her dewlapped neck sounded more like an electric power line.

How strange, I thought, this woman's presence near such a terrible, noxious swamp, for she was frail, homely, her crooked form like that of an armadillo rising to its haunches. Her eyes were bulbous, intense, the outer whites thick with veins that came and went like tiny bursts of lightning. Yet regardless of her appearance, I felt drawn to her, safe even, despite the fact that she slurped and drooled while helping me to my shoeless feet.

As we trudged away from that vile swamp to a nearby path—where the pines still creaked but fog no longer violated our hair—the old woman began pulling stones from the pockets of her garment and hurling them into the forest. Squat green lizards leapt from fallen logs to avoid being hit by the projectiles, their red eyes flashing like the brake lights of cars, a large coin protruding from each flat mouth.

I grasped the woman's skeletal hand. "Hey, that's GOLD!" I said. "Why are you scaring them away?"

Again, no reply. Instead she yanked at the crutch of my arm and we continued on in silence, the moon arcing high overhead as it shuffled the forest shadows.

A crumbling stone cottage soon came into view, its cracked windows aglow with dim lanterns that prodded at the encroaching darkness. We stepped through the open door and the hunchback led me to an old, medieval-looking chair at the center of the living room and nudged me into it. A fire crackled in the stone hearth. Around me the bare, spider-infested interior seemed uninhabited, though a stench, not unlike rotten meat, permeated the air.

Dehydrated, I inquired about a glass of water. "Ma'am, if I could trouble you for—"

This seemed to trigger the appearance of four slithering ropes from a shadowy, cobwebbed corner. They rose off the floor like cobras, then quickly secured my arms and legs to the chair. A black cauldron materialized over the fire. Dream or no dream, I was terrified, and so pleaded with the old hag to let me go. "My good woman, please!" But the crooked thing turned away, her head hidden behind that large hump. And then a cat of the most unkempt black fur, licking the red-stained claws of one tightly curled paw, appeared to my left. That's when the awful question arose in my mind: Were these creatures going to eat me?

That really got me struggling, which in turn got the cat howling. The hunchback then wobbled up to me and started to gnaw at my chest with her toothless gums. I was ready to scream at a volume detrimental to my vocal chords when the floorboards ahead of me cracked apart and fell away, uncovering the gaping mouth of a large, moss-lipped hole.

A pair of white eyes appeared in the dark opening.

Whatever the thing was, it did not reveal itself. Instead a massive tentacle shot out of the opening and slapped against my chest, where it remained. I screamed for help but my captor was dancing a jig, her hair writhing about in the likeness of a gorgon. Nearby, the cat sat stiff on its haunches, its neck unnaturally elongated like a giraffe which it held at a forty-five degree angle toward the hole—the freakish creation of some insane taxidermist. A fly crawled inside the frozen animal's wide-open mouth, stopping on occasion to taste the landscape with its proboscis.

By now the tentacle had shot some kind of liquid into my bloodstream, a bluish secretion I watched drip from a small, retracting stinger. The tentacle then slithered back into the hole, and darkness sealed itself over me like tar.

My next experience took the form of an intense, recurring nightmare, one in which I found myself running through the streets of my city beneath leaning skyscrapers. Windows shattered overhead, raining shards of glass while the open hoods of cars shot out $100 bills. I screamed as falling glass sliced me apart like deli meat, layer by layer.

The dream repeated multiple times, always with another few layers of my body being sliced away by the falling glass. By the end of the final dream I was nothing more than a conscious thread of animated flesh crawling through the smog of the city, a six foot worm. And like a worm, I seemed to be in search of a puddle of muck to drown in.

When at last I awoke—perhaps hours later, I had no way of knowing—I was lying naked on a log-frame bed, hunchback and filthy cat nowhere to be seen. But someone had recently been there, for, in addition to the bed, the interior of the cottage was now adorned with paintings, chairs, and other simple furnishings. Sunlight poured in through the windows, and classic literature and poetry lined the bookshelves. Furthermore, an abundance of canned goods were stacked neatly inside the open kitchen cabinets, while a bowl of fresh fruit sat on a small table beneath the kitchen window.

Tying on a robe left hanging on a hook, and prodded along by rising hunger pangs, I shuffled over to the bowl of fruit and snatched an apple. The moment I bit into it I began to cough. This led to a coughing fit, which lasted for several minutes until I gagged out a long, flowing cloud of—car exhaust!

What followed next can only be described as a surreal deluge of modernity.

First I puked out my wallet, car keys, and wrist watch, these trailed by long wires with electrical outlets at their ends. Worming through this clunky release were myriad sounds and smells—the din of traffic, the odors of fast food burgers, various commercial jingles, the sound alerts of incoming messages. And as I spat out bits of plastic between final gags, an iridescent cloud of polluted air rose out of my throat and spread across the ceiling.

The attack was far from over. I was struck again, this time more violently. It was as if my body had some desperate need to purge itself of its former prison, the city, like a gorilla trying to kick and claw its way through the walls of a zoo.

Suddenly my throat expanded and I spat out batteries, video games, DVDs, my cell phone, and larger items like balls of computer chips. It was very uncomfortable, though I never felt any pain.

When at last the bizarre heaving came to an end, I glanced out the window and noticed a wooden flowerbox, its shriveled petunias beginning to rise and bloom. Just then the front door creaked open with a flood of light, and in trotted a gray cat, clean and loudly purring. The cat was followed in by a beautiful young woman in a yellow sundress.

I straightened my tired body and smiled, then moved to greet her, my need to be social now quite acute. As I did so, the bile-covered cell phone in the pile of expelled items began to ring. This stopped me dead in my tracks. Instinctively, I began to turn around. At this the cat's back rose like a shark fin, and the woman scowled at me with the intensity of a wolf.

I held up a finger, and, without a word, backtracked to the pile of junk and pulled out the phone. I thought, could it be a family emergency? My boss with a new deadline? Perhaps someone who could explain this crazy delusion? But I really had no way of knowing, for the screen did not display a number.

Outside, the sunlight grew dim as if blocked by a passing cloud. I looked over, saw the petunias in the flowerbox droop and fade. A butterfly gliding nearby burst into dust, and the fruit in the bowl turned to mold, the mush beneath twitchy with maggots.

Still I held the phone. I couldn't seem to put it down!

This triggered a terrible reaction in the woman, whose eyes suddenly popped out of her head, rolled up to the wall, and turned into salamanders. Next, her head decomposed down to the skull, her long hair smacking the floor like a wet mop. The woman then went limp as she twisted to the ground, morphing into a fetid puddle of swamp muck full of wiggling mosquito larvae. The cat hissed and scratched at the air, and a moment later its body jerked in multiple directions as it collapsed to the floor in a lifeless heap.

I stepped back and glared down at the phone; the call was still coming in, and I had an overwhelming *need* to answer it. But why not? Wasn't this all just a dream?

I pushed the button and brought the phone to my ear. "Hello?"

A terrible scream burst through the earpiece like a firecracker. Tortured voices arose behind it, these mingled with the barks and howls of some diabolical beast. Something cracked like a whip, and the phone morphed into a screeching bat. The animal wiggled angrily out of my hand, then crashed through the nearby window where it fell into the flowerbox and died. The petunias, in turn, puked out their nectar.

And then the floorboards in front of me dropped out. And again those orb-like eyes floated up and up through the darkness. I knew right then from where that phone call had come.

Meanwhile in the muck puddle, a wispy, rising form began to materialize, its wet hair quickly growing beyond the length of the humpbacked body. The gray fur of the dead cat blackened, while its bones reassembled and propped up the shaky corpse, those tiny jaws chomping madly as if eating taffy. Beneath the cauldron, the logs ignited with a loud burst, and the knives over the mantle trembled and smacked the cottage walls with a kind of inanimate anticipation that raised the hair on my arms. Two pallid gray tentacles, tightly covered in screaming, fiery maws, rose from the hole and slithered toward me.

I bolted for the door, tripping over the emaciated, extended arm of the grotesque hunchback as she glared up at me with bulging eyes, her fat blue tongue swirling over the lips of an exaggerated mouth full of alligator-like teeth tinged red. I grabbed a nearby chair and pulled myself up, then leapt forward and flew out the cottage door into a full-on lightning storm. I ran as fast as I could, bolts exploding all around me, running as if the last train bound for reality was about to leave the station forever.

Down I went, sliding and falling through that awful forest of dark pines and twirling red will-o'-the-wisps, all the way back to the familiar smog of my city, its filthy streets swamped with broken glass and money and all the things I had come to love and despise; all that I had come to depend on.

I've not been able to leave it since.

# The Politician's New Heart

His donor had danced the bogs of Ireland. Had swum the starlit waves of rocky shores. She was optimistic, despite sea rise and the quieting of birds. Despite parched orchids and disenchanted trees. To the end her mind stayed sharp, and her heart beat strong—a true denizen of the hills, hawthorns, and sea.

Today that heart beats in the politician's chest, threading an elder light through modern veins. New thoughts arise in him daily: of the coexistence of enchanted trees and paved roads, of laws cast against the rising seas, of the integration of elemental wisdom. And a new campaign speech forms in his mind—its words free of pollution, and boldly green.

# Post-Funeral Mission to Mars

As the airplane enters the towering clouds, Billy spies wispy ghosts and shifting white valleys. What is turbulence to everyone else, to Billy is an angry fog monster.

An old woman snores beside him. Others resign to airport novels, electronics, and the anticipation of the cart. Humming engines and whooshing air vents backdrop the cries of a baby, of two teenage girls absorbed in gossip.

Billy peers out the cold, turbid window and sees Harryhausen beasts run amok in the cloudscape: dinosaurs gnawing on cars and bridges, a distant Cyclops ripping a train off its tracks.

A break in the clouds reveals a stretch of suburbia, of baseball fields where an interest in sports fell short of home plate. All around, long thin roads blink with ant-cars: "Ants can lift fifty times their own weight, you know," his mother once said, shortly before her funeral.

The edge of an upcoming cirrus cloud swirls over the wings: here comes Conan through the smoke of battle, sword dripping with ruddy sunlight. Bones sail through the fog as he charges an army of skeletons.

Suburbia slides back into view, its rooftops the color of cigarette ash, a string of retention ponds like chicory weeds in cracked pavement. His estranged father intrudes upon his thoughts: "Earth to Billy, Earth to Billy—I said grab me another beer!"

He pulls out a book by Ray Bradbury. After reading a few of his favorite stories he returns to the window, where Charles Knight mammoths [ding] struggle in [ding] tar pits [ding]: *"Ladies and gentlemen, this is your captain speaking. Please fasten your seat belts and turn off all electronics. We'll be landing shortly. Thank you, and have a great day."*

People gather personal items and shut off devices. The woman beside him begins to stir. Tears fill the boy's eyes; he cannot bear to live with his father again. He turns to the window, where his mother's face takes shape in the cloudscape.

"You can go *anywhere*, Billy, anywhere at all," she used to say. "Just hook your imagination to the stars!"

A fiery sunset now paints the clouds, and Billy wipes away his tears. A voice explodes from the intercom static: *"Mars to Billy . . . —ars to Billy . . . This is your mother . . . —der alien attack! I repeat, we're under —n attack! . . . Please—ome to Mars at once. We need your help!"*

The plane morphs into a silver rocket. A space suit drops from an overhead compartment. Billy squeezes past the old woman to the aisle, climbs into the suit, snaps on the helmet. Passengers dissolve as he enters the cockpit. Outside, a star breaks through the clouds.

# Intimate Universes

*Inspired by the theory that cosmic branes (of a multiverse) can touch and influence one another*

Their "kiss" lasted but one millionth of a second,
though truly timeless and spared of angels; a mere gleam
in the dreaming eye of Pan; the first quiver of life in primordial ooze.
A singularity popped off the tongue of a howling black hole,
expanded where nascent gods toss rose petals over looping,
cosmic currents, shot plasma-fire blue into the nothing of our universe—
a universe silent as an ash-covered opera—until the chaos of cooling atoms
induced space-time and spark, lending symphonic gravity
to the tenacity of evolution, to the intangibles of consciousness.

# Penumbra

A series of intensifying tremors shook the foundation of the farmstead, sending workers fleeing in all directions. An eclipse darkened the sky, and long shadows drifted across the windmill, trees, and barns. Moments later, when the tremors subsided, a thin body fell from the sky and landed behind a grain silo.

A young slave, having seen the body fall, sensed something familiar in its aspect and ran toward it. She wasn't the only witness. Three guards had also observed the falling figure, had even seen it hit the ground before *instantly springing to its feet*. The figure then disappeared through the entrance of an underground storage chamber. What concerned the guards most, however, was not that the body had survived the long fall, but that it was significantly larger than them, was the color of a slave, and, most troublesome of all, bore a pair of wings. As it was their duty to protect the settlement, the three guards quickly moved to track down and eliminate the possible threat.

Meanwhile the eclipse persisted, and the farmhands, by nature skittish, chose to remain in hiding until signaled back to work. The guards, on the other hand, continued their pursuit of the winged creature down a subterranean tunnel, unaware that the curious slave was following them.

The guards soon reached the storage chamber and peered inside: the creature was at the far end, clawing frantically at the dirt wall. They entered discreetly, but the thing sensed them and turned around, popping open its wings and enlarging itself. Just then, a stream of chaotic vibrations burst through the sky, and the guards, in a quick, coordinated move, closed in on their target like a pack of wolves.

Several minutes later a guard stumbled out of the chamber and collapsed in front of the slave. The slave stepped around the body and entered the room. There she witnessed a figure pressed firmly against the far wall, its large wings contorted and severely damaged, its limbs twitching silently, mouth agape and oozing fluid. The thing had defended itself vigorously—two of the guards having succumbed to bodily gashes in the chamber while the third had died in the tunnel. The slave cautiously approached the winged creature and looked it over. It appeared to be dead, and it was female.

The slave remained by the corpse for a long time. Though different from her, she couldn't help but register a kinship with it. For one, the color of its skin was the same as hers. There were other similarities as well, and this affected the young slave greatly; so much so, in fact, that she sensed an influx of strange knowledge that shifted her instincts. Soon it became obvious that she did not come from or belong in the settlement.

The slave eventually left the chamber and returned to the surface. By now the eclipse had passed, and most of the farmhands had returned to their assigned labors.

A second eclipse occurred a short time later, again preceded by a series of intensifying tremors. By now the slave had revolted against her captors and was hiding atop a barn, a dying guard in her murderous grasp. She was gazing intently at the sky, trying to make sense of what she saw there: a giant, gruesome head topped with a thick mass of limp antennae; three dark openings beneath a set of what she believed to be eyes; and a wide, rounded body from which dangled two long limbs that sank beneath the horizon. The whole thing swayed back and forth ever so slightly, allowing random beams of sunlight to shoot out from behind its immense form. This, she now realized, was the thing that had dropped her within the tall, transparent walls of the farmstead, the being that had taken her from her home, from her own kind.

And now, the lower opening on the creature's face began to expand and contort, releasing a bizarre stream of vibrations that the slave could not decipher. A long appendage rose into the air holding a rounded container, and this the creature flipped upside down, dropping dozens of familiar bodies into the narrow landscape of the farmstead.

The slave, watching this, tossed aside the dead guard and ran down the side of the barn as quickly as she could. The time had come to unite.

# The Unfortunate Heartbreak of Faritook the Earwig

Faritook stood on an old rotten log in the woods, cleaning one of his antennae. Shanamook was about to come along at any moment, and he knew he had to look his absolute best if she were to stop and talk with him. When she finally emerged from the decaying bark, Faritook released his antenna and edged closer to where she would pass.

But Shanamook shuddered when she saw him. She was creeped out by Faritook, uncomfortable with how he always stared at her, his mandibles moving as if eating something invisible. And though they had seen each other a few times in passing, nothing more had ever transpired between them. They were just two earwigs that passed on the log.

Faritook became increasingly nervous as she got closer, his prepared compliment ready to be spoken. But Shanamook was desperate to make him understand that she just wasn't interested. An idea came to her, one she knew would forever rattle Faritook's central nerve cord: she casually plopped her abdomen against the bark and excreted explosively (causing a nearby centipede to bolt away screaming). After wiggling out the last of it she proceeded on her way, convinced Faritook would no longer have *any* interest in her.

But Faritook did not seem to notice. In fact, he appeared more smitten than ever. "Hello Shanamook!" he said as she passed, his antennae twirling with excitement. "You're looking quite lovely this afternoon."

Shanamook's compound eyes double bugged out. Say what? Did he actually *like* that? Shanamook was in total disbelief. And since she was unable to come up with an appropriate response, she simply sped away. What else could she do? After reaching the orange fungi at the center of the log she glanced back: Faritook just stood there, mandibles extended, staring at her cerci. "What a roach!" she clicked to herself.

After Shanamook disappeared behind the fungi, Faritook dropped into a nearby fissure. There he paced the length of it, dragging his antennae as he tried to figure out what he'd done wrong (the image of her untimely excretion now a suppressed memory). Had he not spoken the words correctly, genuinely? Why had she ignored him? Was it his looks?

Faritook got an idea and ran back to his bachelor chamber.

"Where is it? Where is it?" he muttered to himself, using his pincers to toss aside all kinds of crap he'd collected from a nearby house. "I know you're in here somewhere!"

It was only after he'd made a complete mess of the place that he found what he was looking for: a piece of red frill taken from a human's discarded toothpick. He brought it over to a shard of mirror and wrapped it around his neck like a scarf. I look *good*, he thought to himself. Sophisticated. Debonair!

"Now she'll just *have* to stop and talk with me!" he said with confidence.

At about the time Shanamook was due to return, Faritook stood on the earwig trail with his slick new scarf blowing in the wind. "Any minute now," he said with eagerness. But after half an hour, Shanamook had still not returned. Faritook began to worry. Was she lost? Hurt? Drained by a spider? In the belly of a woodpecker?

Faritook cried out: "Shanamook, where are you? Why have you not returned?"

A passing banana slug stopped in front of Faritook and said, "Hey... Fari... took. Saw... Shana... mook... not... long... ago. She... is... okay. Do... not... worry. She... is... —"

"She's what!" Faritook interrupted.

"She… is… at… —"

"She's at what! Where is she? You fool!"

"Minta… mook's… place," the slug finished.

"Mintamook's place? But what would she be doing at *Mintamook's* place?"

"I… don't… —"

"Never mind!"

"Right. No… time… for… chit… chat," the banana slug went on. "Got… to… be… at… end… of… log… by… twi… light. Sons… of… *bitches*… rac… coons."

But Faritook was already on his way to Mintamook's. And when he arrived a few minutes later he noticed a very peculiar thing: the hole leading to Mintamook's chamber was stuffed with moss. That's odd, Faritook thought, it doesn't look like it's going to rain.

A long moan sounded from deep within the log. "Shanamook!" Faritook gasped. "What is Mintamook *doing* to you!"

But Faritook knew. Knew because he had seen it all before: the cruelty of his species, the pain they often inflicted upon one other. Yes, Faritook knew—knew that his beloved Shanamook was being tortured in the dark wet depths of the underbark!

"I'll save you!" Faritook yelled as he pried out the moss with his pincers. As soon as the hole was open he leapt into the corridor, fully determined to be Shanamook's hero. Light at the far end fluctuated with movement, and Faritook sped toward it through the glow of dead fireflies, which were scattered at intervals along the tunnel. When he finally reached the chamber he enlarged himself and burst in.

"Take your filthy legs off her, you damn dirty bug!"

Both Shanamook and Mintamook turned their heads with a screech, their antennae shooting straight up into the air. But Faritook screeched the loudest, for Shanamook sat limberly on a patch of moss, her six legs spread eagle, Mintamook crouched down in front of her ovipositor.

"Get the hell *out* of here, Faritook!" Shanamook yelled.

"Or I'll tear your puny thorax out!" Mintamook added, opening her pincers.

Unable to regain his composure, Faritook turned and ran down the corridor as fast as he could—completely confused, totally heartbroken, his reproductive organ stiff as a rose thorn.

# Red Icicles

A rare ice storm hit East Tennessee this morning, shutting down schools and causing car wrecks. It was quite beautiful though: a landscape of silver coated trees beneath a stretch of blue mountains. Countless icicles hung from telephone wires and the eaves of houses and shacks. Many folks were out taking photos.

But the storm wasn't much of an inconvenience for me— I'm a writer, I work at home. And in that respect the morning was just like any other.

That is, until about 9:30.

I was hunkered down in my writing room at the time, the location of all my books, movie posters, and monster toys— action figures, I mean—editing a short story. That's when a series of small bangs arose from the kitchen area of my prefab house.

"What the hell is *that?*" I said, glancing at the Wolf Man.

I walked out into the living room, mug of cold coffee in hand, eyes half shut beneath an uncombed head of hair. I made a right turn at the dining area—a spacious extension of the kitchen—and faced the sliding doors of the back patio. There, a bright red cardinal was flying against the glass.

"Dude," I said. "What are you *doing?*"

The cardinal dropped onto a patch of snow, limp and exhausted.

"Don't kill yourself, bird brain," I said to it through the glass.

I wasn't too concerned though, as birds, especially cardinals, had a habit of starting fights with their own reflections. A territorial thing. And they never seemed to truly injure themselves in the process.

I glanced at the microwave clock and groaned—it was too early for a beer. So I shuffled back to the writing room and took a moment to admire my favorite zombie action figure. That's when a series of louder bangs began.

"Here we go again," I said to the zombie. "Bird braaains," I imagined the zombie saying back.

This time, about a dozen birds were whacking themselves against the patio doors. *Pop*, went a sparrow. *Pop*, a wren. *Pop-pop*, a pair of titmice.

"What the hell?"

I looked slightly to my left. Frankenwhiskers, my tiger striped cat, was staring at the lower cabinet where I kept his food.

"Don't you *see* this shit, Frank?"

That's when I noticed the birdfeeder I'd hung off the back eave: it was completely iced over, the tasty morsels trapped inside. And it was nearly empty.

"Is that what you're all so creased about? Can't get to the birdseed? Well that's a dumb reason to bang your skulls against my window!"

Frankenwhiskers walked up to me and began figure 8-ing between my legs. If I didn't feed him soon he'd open the cabinet with his paw and start biting the cat food bag. That's when it occurred to me: the birds wanted *inside* the house, they wanted the birdseed that was in the plastic green bin near the patio doors. No doubt they'd seen me open it each time I refilled the feeder.

"Okay, just calm down," I said to the birds. "Sheesh!"

As I searched around for something to break the ice with, a pair of mockingbirds flew up and began hopping along the patio doors, chattering to one another as they peered into the house. A moment later the phone rang: my lovely fiancée calling from Chicago where she was attending a conference.

"How's the writing going?" she asked.

I may have lied when I assured her it was going "super superbly." She hadn't laughed at that. What did make her laugh, however, was my "story" about the birds.

"It's true!" I said. "Here, listen." I put the phone next to the patio doors but all was silent. The birds had gone. "Ah hell, you bastards."

"Okay, well, see you in a couple of days then," she said. "Love you."

"Love you too."

After feeding the cat, I got distracted by another call and then went back to the writing room. Somehow I had forgotten all about the birdfeeder. For the next couple of hours I was pretty much unaware of anything but my story, though I did hear pitter-patter on the roof now and then, and the cracking of ice.

By noon I was back in the kitchen, engaged in a tasty PBR/PB&J combo. As I went to crack open the beer, a windowpane shattered and a long stream of birds came rushing into the house—all with sharp icicles in their beaks. Frankenwhiskers meowed "Shit!" and ran behind the couch. Pussy.

"Whoa, wait a minute. Waaait a minute!" I announced to the Hitchcockian gathering, bits of sandwich tumbling from my mouth. A crow swooped in and landed atop the birdseed bin where it began to tap the lid with its icicle. "Okay, okay, I get it—you're hungry. No problem!"

I inched my way toward the birdseed bin, eyeing each bird cautiously as I went. Some were perched on chairs and cabinets, others stood directly on the counter, their icicles pointed forward. A turkey—seriously, a *turkey?*—poked its head through the broken window holding a large, double-spiked icicle of its own. The mockingbirds from earlier zipped past me and landed on the floor next to the couch.

As I reached down for the bin, the crow lifted off and flew up to the kitchen table. There it puffed up its chest, gave me the cold eye, then "sharpened" its icicle on the edge of the table and pooped.

A second later, Frankenwhiskers howled and ran out from behind the couch with two icicles stuck in his back; the mockers had got him. I nearly screamed and made a move to help the poor thing, but the birds were staring me down, heads tilted as if listening to my thumping heart. Silence followed. No sound but the *drip-drip* of a few icicles. So I held my breath, took the lid off the bin, and looked inside.

I was all out of birdseed.

# Ghoul of the Enamel

Tonight we sense him, hidden in the sunken shadows of the bedroom: a ghoul moving silent, forcing quiet the other monsters. Chunks of enamel, grooved by nightly gnawing, fatten his belly. And our own teeth tighten in the jaw, fight the urge to drop and slip away, to escape his gluttonous rage. You see, the foul thing broke from fairy law: took to ripping out the loose teeth of children, a calcareous shit slipped beneath their bloodied pillows in a gesture of defiance; a jab at us proper fairies. And though imprisoned for a time in the amber caves, he broke free—saber arms flapping and chipping with madness.

Now we wait within this toy-box, scanning the room for residual energies: the moans of bloody roots, the chattering of crowns, the hissing red of severed nerves . . . . Such things betray his whereabouts.

At last we fly and crawl from the moonlit box, eyes narrowed and tongues writhing with an invocation. Oh how swift, how *sweet* the coming of revenge from its ancient lair! Soon the children will sleep soundly; they'll remember nothing of the ghoul. Money will be dispersed where due, and the status of the tooth fairy will be restored to its innocuous state. Because tonight we are going to pounce on the fiend. Unravel his existence. Shred into his stomach and take back what is ours.

# Deal Down at the Hospital

"After I died," said seven-year-old Cassie, suddenly free of cancer and wild in the eyes, "there was a big red sky with a *huge* head floating in it like . . . like the *moon,* only super close. It was a' old man, like a wizard, with sharp teeth a thousand feet high and gray lips and *no* hair—not even eyebrows—and his eyes, they were all white, and they looked sleepy."

The little girl bounced on the hospital bed, feet dangling beneath her gown. She tilted her head and pinched at her hair, which was just starting to regrow. She couldn't wait to get her pigtails back.

"And he, and he *drooled* a lot too," she went on, "like waterfalls that fell forever. And there were white fuzzies floating into his mouth. It was all dark in there, except in the back where it glowed orange."

She paused, clawing thoughtfully at her gown. Her bright eyes danced along with the memories as they came rushing back.

"Oh yeah, and there were all these little funny-looking heads going around the big head like . . . like meteors. They were spinning and going round and round and laughing. They were so happy!"

"Mm-hm," said the doctor, distracted as he went back and forth between various charts and x-rays. "Go on."

"Then the wizard head *talked,* but not with his mouth though. His mouth was open the whole time like a stinky cave. But all the words went right into my head like, um, like tel-e . . . tel-e-*path*ic?"

43

"Telepathic—right," replied the doctor, scratching his head over a recent x-ray. His other hand reached for the little girl's knee. She flinched, then quickly stood up on the bed and stretched. "Guess what he said?" she asked, her spine cracking quietly.

"I don't know, honey. Tell me. What did the wizard head say?"

"He said if I want to, I can live to be *two hundred* years old!"

"That was nice of him," said the doctor, biting his lip as he recalled the pattern on her underwear. He politely asked her to sit down, then turned to grab some paperwork. The little girl giggled and reached for a nearby scalpel, her thin shadow stretching across the man's white lab coat. She bent her knees and leaned forward, swaying from side to side like a parakeet about to fly out of an open cage.

"I just have to keep my promise first," she said flatly, raising the scalpel over her head.

"Oh yeah?" said the doctor. "What's that?"

After she leapt onto the floor and crawled between the man's legs, the little girl wasted no time in fulfilling her promise that the bad man would never become aroused again.

# The Tramp Clown's Secret

The sky was clear, the moon nearly full. Fireflies rose from the gardens and drifted over manicured lawns where old timers, arm in arm with nurses or slumped forward in wheelchairs, returned from late afternoon strolls. Two male residents sat on the porch of the nursing home in flannel shirts and overalls, sipping chamomile tea in their rockers. They had spent the last few hours catching up, as they had not seen each other in sixty years.

"I really do miss her," Sam muttered, eyes moist and red beneath his flat cap.

Virgil stopped rocking and leaned sideways over the small wicker table between them. "What's that you say?"

Sam raised his mucus-lined voice. "*Ruthie*. I miss Ruthie."

"Oh."

Sam stared into his mug as if hypnotized by a vision there, the lines of his face deep enough to hold thin shadows. He opened his mouth to speak, then thought the better of it. Finally he put his tea down and said, "Virgil, there's somethin' I've been meanin' to ask you for sixty years now."

"Yea? What's that?" Virgil's voice was gravelly.

"Well . . . You left Rockford the day after Ruthie was killed. You didn't tell anyone where you were going, not even *me*, and we were friends. That was awfully strange of you."

Virgil, an overweight man in his early eighties, dragged a square-ended fingernail across the armrest of his rocker. "We went over this already, Sam. I told you: the circus offered me a full-time gig."

Sam waved off a mosquito. "Mm-hmm. And why'd you wait sixty years to come back? The *real* reason. You don't expect me to believe you simply wanted to live out your days in Rockford, do you?" He snickered. "No-no—I think you came back to get somethin' off your conscience."

"Get *what* off my conscience?"

Sam's face turned red. "You didn't even stay long enough to see Ruthie put in the ground!"

Virgil scanned the floorboards at his feet. "I told you, Sam. There just wasn't nothin' left for me here. We weren't even speakin' at the time, so what did it matter? And what choice did I have? Tramp clown's all I was ever good at. I belonged with the circus; that was my true home." He licked spittle from the corners of his mouth. "Sorry I didn't say goodbye. Or keep in touch. I didn't know how, Sam. Truly."

Sam shook his head in disapproval. "You didn't even come back for your *brother's* funeral," he huffed, intent on prodding the man. "Surly you knew of his murder."

Virgil took a deep, wheezy breath and sipped his tea, the face of his twelve-year-old brother lingering inside his mind. He looked out along the darkening pathways of the property, at the nurses, the slow-moving residents in their white gowns, and imagined Miles, his younger brother, sprinting in circles around them, making fun. His eyes watered. "I guess I couldn't face that, either. I was a coward."

The porch light flicked on and a young nurse stuck her head out from behind the screen door, releasing a lavender fragrance into the air. "You two alright out here?" she asked.

"What?" Virgil had an ear toward the nurse. A moth shot over his puffy white hair and bounced off the light.

"We're alright, Miss Ramsey," Sam said, winking at her. "Don't wait up."

The nurse raised an eyebrow. "Be sure to stay on the porch, guys. Okay? I'll be back later to check on you. In the meantime, be good."

The men grinned with their fake teeth and the nurse left smiling.

"You didn't buy that story about Thompson, did you?" Sam went on, turning to Virgil with crossed arms.

"The drifter? Who else? He confessed to everything."

"What if the police forced him to sign that confession? There wasn't a shred of evidence linking him to the crimes. And besides, Ruthie was murdered in late June, Miles early July. Yet no one reported seeing Thompson around until *mid*-July. I think he died in prison an innocent man."

Virgil belched abruptly and said, "What on earth are you getting at?"

Sam sighed. He reached for his tea, sipped it, then shakily placed it back on the wicker table. "Well, since you can't see where I'm goin' with all this, then I'll just have to come right out and say it. Besides, I've got angina and I can't bear the stress. No more secrets."

"Secrets?" Virgil was taken aback.

Sam looked around to be sure no one was within earshot, then stared at Virgil with his steel blue eyes, the only part of him that retained a youthful quality. "I suspected you all along," he said.

"What? Speak up, Sam. I can't hear you."

Sam smacked the armrest. "Ruthie. You murdered her!"

"What? That's preposterous!" Virgil said.

"You were jealous she chose me over you, so you killed her. Then you took your clown act and hooked up with the circus— a *traveling* circus, I might add—knowing damn well you had a job waiting for you down at the mill, here, with me. But you were hiding, weren't you? And why was that? Because you were *guilty*, that's why. We both know Ruthie would never have gone into those woods with that drifter. But she trusted *you*, Virgil, and you killed her."

Unsure how to reply, Virgil could only stare at his old friend.

"So maybe you're wonderin' why I didn't turn you in," Sam said, removing his flat cap and wiping sweat off his bald head. "Well, I'll tell you." He replaced the hat and reached around for his wallet. "Because I decided to get even, that's why." He pulled out a pair of thick glasses from the breast pocket of his overalls and placed them low on his nose. A tattered baseball card was taken from the wallet. After admiring it for a few moments he raised his eyebrows and said, "Great player."

He passed the card to Virgil, whose face dropped like a cannonball.

"Your brother's favorite player," Sam said with a smirk, leaning in toward his old friend. "And it's signed, too. See? Miles never went anywhere without that card."

Virgil stared intensely at his dead brother's baseball card, his lower lip trembling.

"Are you tellin' me that . . . that it was *you* who murdered Miles?" Virgil said, eyes still on the card. "That you murdered my brother because . . . because you thought I killed Ruthie?"

Sam pinched a mosquito off his liver-spotted arm and rolled it between his fingers, popping out the blood. "Well—you *did*, didn't you?" He looked out across the deserted lawn, crinkling his forehead. Katydids sang from a nearby patch of woods. "I mean . . . you hated us for dating. You can't deny that." His eyes narrowed as he searched the dusty shelves of his memory for additional evidence. "I'll never forget that day at the circus," he went on, "your first show here in Rockford, the day Ruthie died. We came to congratulate you after the performance, but you turned away. Ruthie grabbed you by the sleeve and you spun around with the most *hateful* look I'd ever seen on a man. It showed right through your makeup. I knew right then what you were capable of."

Virgil continued to stare at the baseball card. His face began to go pale and his pot belly heaved. "I need to lie down," he said, rising from his rocker. "I don't feel well." He slid the card into the hip pocket of his overalls and shuffled past Sam to the screen door.

"You ain't gonna call the cops, are you?"

"No, Sam," Virgil said in a low voice, "I'm not gonna call the cops. They wouldn't bother with all this now anyway." He shut the door behind him.

Chest pain seized Sam's tongue before he had a chance to reply. He wanted to take it all back, to right the situation by telling Virgil he was only testing him to see what he'd say. Instead he closed his eyes and let the angina run its course. In his mind, he and Ruthie walked down Main Street together, laughing and kissing and getting to know each other. She had a freshly picked daisy over her left ear and a green ribbon at the end of her braided ponytail . . . .

Overhead, the moon arced its way across a darkening sky. Somewhere in the distance a whip-poor-will began its nocturnal lament. The screen door creaked open and a disheveled, overweight man shambled onto the porch. His gray suit, covered in patches, and which he'd obviously outgrown in every direction, fell in tatters, its pockets attached with safety pins. The man wore a brown derby, red clown nose, and had white makeup around his mouth where sloppy greasepaint mimicked a five o'clock shadow. An oversized polka-dot tie hung loosely at the collar of a grimy white shirt, and coarse chest hair squiggled out from openings where buttons were missing. He sat down in Virgil's chair and began to rock, his demeanor theatrically downtrodden.

Sam woke with a start and rushed his hands across his face, sending off mosquitoes. He looked over and saw a green ribbon lying on the wicker table. It was tied to a braid of brown hair.

A thick hand popped into the space over the braid. The hand, covered by a wool glove with the fingers cut out, flicked open and rotated above the hair as if presenting a crystal ball. Sam looked up to see a tramp clown sitting in Virgil's rocker.

"Virgil!" Sam exclaimed, propping himself up. His eyes darted numerous times between the clown and the braid of hair. "W-what is this? Is that—? Why are you dressed as Garbo? Tell me this instant! Why—?"

Realization suddenly flashed across his eyes, and he scowled furiously. "O-o-h, I get it," he fumed, shaking a crooked finger at the clown. "It was *you* all along, wasn't it? *Garbo's* the one killed Ruthie." He lifted his chest. "I suppose that makes *you* innocent, is that right? Well guess what, you deaf old fool—you can pin your murder on Garbo, but it won't clear you in the eyes of the Lord. Or me!"

Garbo, his face expressing deep sadness, nodded in agreement.

Sam clenched his arthritic fists and set a marble-hard gaze on the clown. "You're gonna *burn* in hell, Virgil," he coughed, his chest pain returning.

Garbo turned an ear toward Sam and cupped his hand around it.

"I said, 'You're gonna *burn* in hell'! And guess who'll be right there beside you? That's right—*me*." His eyes were filled with angry tears. "Why? Because we're *child* killers, Virgil. The worst there is. You and I, we're gonna burn—"

The clown stuck his fingers into his ears and clacked his tongue. Sam reached over and yanked one of his arms. "Now you stop that!"

Garbo sighed dramatically, then reached into his tattered suit and pulled out a long carving knife, turning it from side to side as if trying to read its future. He placed it gently on the wicker table beside Ruthie's hair. Nocturnal sounds echoed through the gardens and circled the moment. Sam looked down at the knife, then at the braid, then at the knife again. When Garbo turned his head, Sam snatched the knife off the table with both hands and aimed it at the clown, his left arm now throbbing with intense pain.

50

"I should've done this a long time ago, you . . . you *cock*sucker!"

He lunged forward, but the knife slipped out of his hands and he toppled to the ground, clutching at his heart. Garbo tilted his head like a dog and watched it all go down: the convulsions, the bugged-out eyes, the mouth sucking at the air like a landed fish. When it was all over he giggled like a little boy.

By now the moon was illuminating the porch like a lion tamer's spotlight. Garbo squinted, and in the glare found that everything around him—including the nursing home, its grounds, and Sam's motionless body—had faded away, and was being replaced by an old-time circus: a crowded arena of elephants, clowns, jugglers, and trapeze artists.

In response, Garbo jumped to his feet and fell into the old act. He danced, rolled over, walked on his hands, flirted with the girls, threw gag gifts to the boys, his broad grins and heavy frowns evoking laughter and sympathy from the audience. He felt joy like never before. And he didn't forget the important people. No sir. He made sure to wink at Ruthie and Sam, his best friends, and Miles, his little brother, who sat in the front row of the bleachers, cheering him on.

But as quickly as it came, the joy was torn out of his heart, for the performance had come to its scheduled end. The music stopped, the applause faded, lights were shut down, one by one. And as the crowd quickly dispersed, taking Miles, Sam, and Ruthie with it, Garbo reached down for his push broom and began to sweep. He swept at everything in front of him: the debris, the dust, the fading spotlight beneath his tired bones. With heavy shoulders, and a face of perpetual sadness, Garbo sighed as he swept it all away—swept and swept until only he and the knife remained.

# Not for Mortal Eyes

Jen entered the lab holding two large coffees. Her coworker, Edwin, gently set down a beaker of blue liquid and turned around. "Good morning, Dr. Liu," he said, tapping his foot to the jazz tune "Something's Coming" by Dave Grusin. "Ready to capture a few dreams today?"

"Edwin, we've been working together for five years now. If you don't quit with all that 'Doctor' nonsense, I'm going to stop bringing these fancy lattes you love so much." She smiled and offered him a cup. "Just 'Jen,' okay?"

"Hold on," Edwin said. "I'll have to rewire my brain first." With a stroke of his gray beard the scientist stared intently at the ceiling and repeated the words "Just Jen" several times before taking the coffee. Then he winked and said, "Thanks, *Just Jen.*"

Jen rolled her eyes and set her cup down. She grabbed a lab coat off the wall and wrapped it around her petite frame, then paused to wipe her thick-rimmed glasses on the stiff fabric. Edwin glanced sideways at her, appreciating that although she was young, she conducted herself with a maturity and efficiency beyond her twenty-nine years. Her devotion to science had often evoked in him thoughts of the daughter he never had.

"Guess you decided to come in early this fine *Saturday* morning," Jen said, poking fun at him for adding Saturdays to their schedule, not that she had any kind of social life she was missing out on. She paused amid the lab's flurry of activity: microscope illuminators, clunky computers, the sleep lab surveillance monitor, and, of course, the tiny radio tuned to

Edwin's favorite jazz station. Coffee, jazz, and science, he often said, were the only things that kept his "old butt" going. Not even marriage could compete with his unwavering goal to digitally reconstruct a human dream, which, thanks to Jen, was quickly becoming a reality.

And it was all hinged on their serum, a concoction that was becoming increasingly successful at amplifying the electrochemical pathways in dreaming, mammalian brains. In conjunction with a prescribed dose of the blue liquid, receptors on a tiny scanner implanted near the test subject's secondary visual cortex recorded and digitized the amplified brain activity and relayed it back to the central computer; there, data were filtered through a complex program and assembled into static images.

After nearly five years of calibrating various components, including an array of electrodes and other devices, the scientists had finally neared their goal of producing crisp, detailed images from a human dream, the implications of which were certain to unravel many of the brain's mysteries, including consciousness.

"So how's the serum shaping up?" Jen asked, clipping on her university badge.

"Oh, quite nicely. I think there's a chance for optimal results by late morning." The elder scientist handed Jen some papers scribbled with formulas and notes. "Just modify the serum as indicated here—see, at the bottom there—then we'll run some tests before Jim gets in."

"Jim's in today?" Jen sighed. "Sometimes he makes me miss the rats."

"We've come a long way from testing on rats," Edwin said. "I for one was getting tired of endless dream captures of fuzzy maze walls and cheese." He laughed.

"I know, I know. I was only kidding. Really. I'm glad you found him. It's just . . . well, never mind." Sensing a slight flush in her cheeks, Jen scrunched her forehead and quickly flipped through the pages of the revised serum. "Wow, this could be the one we've been waiting for," she said. "This could work!" And although she secretly despised Edwin's jazz, her fingers snapped along with the music as she walked over to her work station at the other end of the lab.

A short time later Jim Coal, their test subject, began to wake from a state of deep sleep in a lab down the hall, dozens of multi-colored electrodes webbed over his head.

"Dr.—er, Jen, come take a look at this." It was Edwin calling from the computer desk. Jen came up behind him and leaned over his shoulder, arms folded across her chest. "What is it?"

"That last batch of serum . . . well, here—just look." He pointed to a slightly blurry, colorized image on the computer screen; a digital capture from Jim's dream. "See that? Doesn't that sort of look like—?"

"Jim's father!" Jen gasped. "That looks a hell of a lot like Jim Sr."

Edwin held up a black & white photograph from Jim's file. It showed Jim in a Little League uniform, his father standing to his right, a possessive hand on the boy's slumped shoulder. The man wore a military style haircut.

Jen bit her bottom lip to contain her excitement. "I can't believe it," she said. "This is without a doubt the *best* image we've ever gotten!"

"Yes, the serum's much improved," Edwin said. "But I think we can do better." He tapped the desk with his fingers and scrutinized the image. "Another hour or so of tweaking should do the trick."

Jen grabbed his hand and squeezed it. "I'll go see if Jim's willing to stay a bit longer." She turned and rushed out the door.

Meanwhile, Edwin grew thoughtful as he further compared the man in the photograph to the one on screen. Both images clearly showed the same person—a tall, imposing figure with broad shoulders, square jaw, and close-set eyes.

According to Jim, his father had been physically and emotionally abusive to both him and his mother. His mother, too afraid to divorce the man, had taken the brunt of the abuse. Then, one morning, as if by answered prayers, his father's smoking corpse was discovered in the woods behind the family home. Although the police had initially suspected foul play, a final report concluded that Jim Sr. had died of self-immolation. The cause: financial-related stress, gambling debts, and other misfortunes. Things might have turned out okay for Jim had it not been for the nightmares, nightmares in which his charred father stalked him in every conceivable setting, nightmares that had grown more realistic and threatening over time.

Those same dreams had been the source of Jim's depression and sporadic employment as an adult. When Edwin first encountered him on a late night walk about town, the man was curled up on a heap of garbage in the yellow spray of an alley light, writhing in the clutches of a nightmare. Edwin shook the man awake to console him, then handed him his number. Jim called a few days later, which led to his becoming a test subject for Edwin's dream project. Edwin *did* fudge facts in the paperwork a bit, choosing not to reveal the man's occasional lack of dependability and frequent benders. But it was Edwin's inclination that Jim's participation would not only help alleviate his vivid, ever-worsening nightmares—in conjunction with therapy, of course—but that it would also produce the best possible results for the experiments because his dreams *were* so vivid. In light of these factors, occasional tardiness and hangovers were tolerated.

Now, after several months of trial and error, Edwin found himself staring at what was once considered a scientific impossibility—an image from the realm of human dream; the image of a man, no less, this one standing in a sort of mist or smoke, his eyes aglow.

\* \* \*

Edwin appeared at the doorway of Jen's office around one o'clock, holding a bottle of cheap champagne and two disposable cups. Jen looked up and swallowed a bite of her sandwich.

"Edwin! Where'd you go, man?" She shoved a romance novel beneath a messy pile of papers as a few breadcrumbs tumbled from her lower lip. "Don't you realize how creepy it is around here when no one's around? I thought you were going to run another test before lunch."

"I did, but this time I wanted to surprise you."

Jen put her sandwich down and glanced at the champagne. "What's *that*, the secret ingredient for perfecting the serum?"

Edwin released two quick grunts that more or less qualified as a laugh. "No, not exactly."

"Good news then! Well, pop that sucker and tell me all about it."

After the champagne was poured, Edwin handed her a cup and then raised his own. "Well, it's been five long years," he said, "but today—"

"So the serum's at optimal performance? You got a focused image in proper color?" Jen's face lit up like a cat watching sparrows at a birdfeeder.

"Yes. Coupled with a larger injection, the upgraded serum worked perfectly. We got a crystal clear image from Jim's most recent dream. His father again, though a bit monstrous this time." He paused. "Hmm. It's unfortunate he hasn't been able to shake off these nightmares about his father. They're actually getting worse, I think."

Jen nodded sympathetically.

"At any rate, everything syncs up now: the serum, the scanner implant, Jim's electrochemical activity. The latest calculations are the magic formula, if you will, and we're getting an image every three and a half seconds. When Jim returns from lunch we'll do a full run, capture an entire dream cycle without interruption."

"That's wonderful, Edwin. We'll get hundreds of successive images!"

"*And*, the first usable dataset for our big paper." Edwin blew out a deep breath. "We did it, Jen. We finally did it. Here's to us. Here's to *dreams*."

"Corny, Edwin, corny," Jen said, clipping his cup, "but I'll play along."

Edwin raised an eyebrow, suddenly hesitant to drink. "Hmm, perhaps we should keep our heads clear." He set his cup on a nearby shelf crammed with scientific journals. Jen lifted hers even higher. "Ah, to hell with it," she said, "we deserve it." She winked at Edwin and gulped down the champagne.

A deep, scratchy voice entered the room. "What do we have here, a celebration?"

"Ah, Jim. Come in," Edwin said, gesturing with his arm.

A lanky man of thirty, with dark stubble and a prematurely aged face, staggered in through the doorway.

Edwin clasped his hands together. "Glad to see you back. How was your lunch break?"

"Meh," Jim said, glancing at Jen. He always looked at Jen, even when answering Edwin's questions. "My headache didn't take much of a break."

"Hold on, I've got some aspirin," Jen said, her voice becoming slightly more feminine. She bent to the lowest drawer of her desk, exposing a hint of cleavage. The look on Jim's face gave the impression that he was imagining her in fewer clothes.

"Nah, I'll be fine," he said, still watching Jen as she put the aspirin back. "This is what I get for sitting at the bar all night."

"Jim," Edwin said, "we've had an incredible breakthrough. We're finally getting the results we've been hoping for! Just a few more sessions and we can talk about extracting that device from your secondary visual cortex. We—"

"My what?" Jim's eyes and mouth slid down together, as if connected.

Edwin put a hairy-knuckled finger to the back of his own head. "Your secondary visual cortex, remember?"

Jim rolled his eyes. "Oh yea, that. Gotcha."

"I know we've kept you in the dark for a long time now," Edwin went on, "so as to not influence the experiments, of course, but very soon we're going to let you in on *all* the details. We've made a magnificent breakthrough, and its implications are going to greatly impact the scientific community, if not the world." He paused for effect. "Don't be surprised if you find yourself quite the celebrity."

"Celebrity?" Jim pointed at his own head. "Visual cortex, the golden fucking egg, right?" He glared at the ceiling, "Hey dad, you catchin' this? These scientists here are gonna make me rich and famous. And you never thought I'd amount to a hill of snake shit, did ya." He snorted to himself.

"You're more than welcome to attend the conferences, too," Jen said. "You know, to tell everyone how we forced you to be our guinea pig." She looked at Edwin and then at Jim, a smile on her face.

"Ah, a guinea pig," Jim said. "I like that. Much cuter than an ol' ugly lab rat, right?" He inflated his cheeks and scratched the stubble on his chin. Jen laughed over her hand to hide one of her bottom teeth, which was crooked.

Edwin held out the sleeping pills he'd produced from his lab coat. "You ready, Jim?" he said.

The man raised his arms in mock surrender. "Alright, alright! Jeez, you scientists—all work and no play." He popped the pills into his mouth and swallowed them without water, then wriggled out of his jean jacket and dumped it on a nearby chair. "I'm all yours," he said, smiling at Jen.

\* \* \*

"Wake him up, wake him up!"

Edwin was shouting as he and Jen burst into the sleep lab. Electrodes were popping off Jim's head in all directions as he thrashed around on the bed. Jen ran up to his side, only to be knocked away by a wild arm, her glasses flying off and hitting the floor. "I said stay away from me!"

Edwin pushed down on Jim's shoulders.

"You're burning in hell!" Jim raged on. "You can't hurt us any—" His eyes suddenly flew open and he glanced around, confused. "What the hell's going on?" Beads of sweat rolled down his forehead.

"You were having a nightmare," Edwin said, catching his breath. He let go of Jim's shoulders. "We've never seen you so upset."

Jen retrieved her glasses and assessed the damage. There was a small vertical crack in one of the lenses.

"Are you okay?" Edwin asked her.

"Yes, you?"

"Fine, fine." He scratched the back of his head. "That must've been some dream, Jim."

Jen put her glasses back on. "I think we should call it a day."

Edwin rested his hands on the back of a nearby chair. "Could this be a side effect of the new serum?"

"I don't think so," Jen said, "but I'll definitely look into it."

Jim labored to sit up, his eyes furtive and glossed over. He shook his head, breathing heavily. "He's comin' for me. Fucker's comin' for me and he ain't gonna stop. I need to get out of here. I need a drink."

"That's not a good idea, Jim," Edwin said. "You need to take it easy for a few minutes. And who? Who's coming for you? Your father?"

Jim squinted at the elder scientist. "You know what, man? I really don't need a therapy session right now. Just leave me the hell alone."

Edwin backed off. "Alright Jim, alright. We'll go. Take as much time as you need. But come and find us as soon as you're ready. I'd like to conduct one more test while we've still got you here. Okay?"

Jen shot Edwin a look, but the scientist had already turned to leave.

"We're going to help you through this," Jen added, putting her hand on Jim's shoulder. "We're going to help you get better." The man shook his head and stared down at the floor.

∗    ∗    ∗

Back in the main lab, Jen and Edwin sat scrolling through a series of incoming images, each a digitized slice of Jim's recent nightmare. Jen opened her notebook. The first image revealed a woman bathing nude inside what appeared to be a large, horizontally-severed cactus. "Um, is that me?" Jen squinted at the screen. "Shit. How embarrassing."

Edwin didn't know what to say, so he remained silent.

Jen focused on the oversized breasts. "Well, at least he compliments me," she said, a bit creeped out. She began to take notes:

IMG-5800: *Dr. Jen Liu bathing nude inside top of large, horizontally-severed cactus in desert landscape.*

IMG-5801: *Water in cactus has turned red. Is this blood?*

IMG-5802: *Hundreds of fissures shooting out from base of cactus in all directions.*

IMG-5803: *Entire image appears to be engulfed in flame.*

IMG-5804 to 5806: *Dark box suspended in space.*

IMG-5807: *Inside a dark room (inside box?), stars and galaxies visible through transparent floor, walls, and ceiling.*

IMG-5808: *Blurry, human-like figure curled up in far corner, heart and veins visible through skin, fire spread across bottom of transparent floor.*

Jen pointed at the figure. "That looks like a child."

Edwin pulled at his beard as he waited for the next image.

IMG-5809: *Entire image has the appearance of fire again.*

IMG-5810 & 5811: *Bluebird on charred wooden floor in an odd "courtship dance"—its wings extended forward.*

"This dream is much more vivid than his recent ones," Edwin said, "and the symbolic imagery quite chaotic and random. Something very interesting is going on with Jim today."

IMG-5812: *Bluebird lifeless, its body twisted in two directions as if mutilated by invisible hands.*

"Ew, that's not nice." Jen grabbed a can of soda off the table and cracked it open.

IMG-5813: *Back inside dark room, figure standing in center, appears to be an adult, flames still visible beneath transparent floor.*

IMG-5814: *Figure closer, resembles a young Jim Coal, looks frightened, gun in right hand, gasoline can in left hand.*

IMG-5815: *Jim standing at edge of woodland with items from previous image.*

IMG-5816: *Entire shot composed of flames.*

IMG-5817 to 5819. *A young Jim smiling (maybe crying), floating in space with hundreds of white butterflies spiraling around him.*

Edwin touched Jen's arm. "Look at this one," he said. "See the time here? This is where he got upset." IMG-5820: *Jim's mouth open as if screaming, butterflies on fire, trees burning in background.*

IMG-5821: *Close-up of Jim Coal Sr. (Jim's deceased father) taking up entire frame, eyes bright red.*

"This is getting horrific!" Jen said.

Edwin's eyebrows shot up. "It's fascinating!"

IMG-5822 & 5823: *Image blurry and unrecognizable.*

IMG-5824: *Another close-up of Jim Sr.'s face, seemingly angry.*

IMG-5825: *Image blurry and unrecognizable.*

The images continued to switch between the blurry and angry close-ups of Jim Sr., representing nearly fifteen seconds of dreamtime.

IMG-5830 (last image before Jim woke up): *Another close-up of Jim Sr.'s face, bordered by fire, mouth wide open and full of sharp teeth.*

Jen dropped her pencil. The computer started beeping.

"Edwin, a new set of images is coming through!"

They turned to the video monitor where Jim could be seen thrashing around on the bed in the sleep lab. "*Dammit!* He must've dozed off," Edwin said, jumping to his feet. "Jen, stay here and get the data saved to the external hard drive, and be sure to keep recording the sleep lab. I'll go help him."

"Edwin, be careful!"

The scientist nodded and took off down the hall. Jen wheeled herself in front of the computer and clicked on the window of incoming images. The first revealed a dark, broad-shouldered figure in an ember-colored haze. The figure materialized as she clicked ahead, its closely set, red eyes seeming to glare right *into* the tiny receptors in Jim's brain. The figure broke forward with each successive image, by degrees becoming the distorted physiognomy of Jim's father. Then, without warning, it took on the gruesome aspect of an archetypal demon.

Jen gasped and knocked over her soda.

Trembling, she continued to click through the images, watching in horror as the creature jumped out of frame, reappearing a few frames later dragging a person, dragging *Jim*, toward a now visible pit of fire. It raised the man high over its head, then tossed him carelessly into the pit with an image-by-image eruption of flame.

A long, terrible scream echoed past the doorway.

Jen jumped up. "What the—!"

Movement on the sleep cam caught her eye: there, in pulsating laboratory light on a blood-soaked bed lay Jim's contorted, lifeless body, a frayed hole where his face used to be. At his side, covered in sizzling chunks of gore, stood the hairless, seven-foot demon from his dream, wisps of steam rising off the naked gray body. Seething red eyes danced in their sockets, while black, human-faced worms slithered maggot-like around its limbs. A grotesquely oversized mouth, with lips rolled back to expose an overabundance of sharp teeth, snapped at the air. By the time it turned to the camera and spoke, Jen was already out the door.

"Not for mortal eyes!" it snarled with a swipe of its hand, killing the video feed.

Jen stopped halfway down the hall and listened for movement. There the demon burst through the swinging doors like a rogue tank. It turned, glared at Jen, then spread its arms to the walls, setting them ablaze. Edwin stumbled out behind it and fell to the floor as smoke billowed from the laboratory.

"Edwin!" Jen cried.

As if carrying out a plan, the demon entered a nearby lab and could be heard destroying it. Jen bolted up to Edwin, who quickly got to his feet and clutched at her lab coat. "Our data!" he whispered harshly, balancing himself. "I've *got* to save our data!"

"But Edwin, that thing!"

"No, Jim's the one it came for."

"But what *is* it?" Jen said as they sprinted back to the main lab.

"Jim's father. Something. I don't know. It just burst through his face. Small at first, then it just . . . grew. From where, I don't know. But I think we've seen too much, Jen. We've seen too much and it's going to destroy everything!" He peered down the hall, eyes frantic. "Get outside, call for help. I'll grab the hard drive and catch up. Go!" He turned and ran into the lab.

By now the demon was charging down the hall like an angry hog. In a panic Jen rushed back into the lab and tried to shut the door, but the creature came up behind her and burst in. Losing her balance, Jen turned and fell against the computer table. The demon took a step forward, but Edwin jumped in front of it and blasted it with a fire extinguisher. Jen leapt out of the way and maneuvered along the wall, holding her breath as waves of heat assaulted her from the doorway. There she paused beneath the billowing smoke as sprinklers rained over the roaring flames.

Edwin made a second dash for the computers. The demon, unfazed by the extinguisher, pulled the human-faced worms off its body and flung them at the equipment. Wriggling, they burst through the hardware with their grotesque heads and slithered inside, sending out sparks and smoke from the holes.

Edwin cursed.

The demon spun around and lowered itself to meet Edwin's face. *"Not for mortal eyes,"* it hissed, inhaling hot saliva through its gray teeth. Then, with a sharp crack of its jaw, the voice turned into that of Jim Sr. "Tell *anyone* about what you saw today," he said, "and I'll haunt you and that bitch for the rest of your lives. *You got that?"*

Edwin turned from its sulfuric breath and coughed. The demon, now laughing, ignored Jen and made its way back through the smoke-filled hallway to the sleep lab. There it shrank with a chaotic blur and climbed back into what remained of Jim's splattered head.

Meanwhile, Jen and Edwin stumbled out of the exit doors and into the flashing lights of emergency vehicles. Jen stopped abruptly, yanking at Edwin's arm. "Delete *everything* from today," she said, her voice trembling. "And destroy every last file on Jim Sr. Okay? We can't risk having that thing come back." Coughing, she pulled the hard drive out of her lab coat and pushed it into Edwin's hands. He stared at it blankly.

"Promise me!" Jen snapped.

Edwin flinched, his fingers gripping the device. "Jen, you did it. You saved our data!"

"Promise me," Jen repeated, still coughing. She locked onto his bloodshot eyes, tears in her own. "Because what if next time that awful thing comes for *us?"*

Edwin turned away, watching the long arcs of water from the fire trucks disappear into the rising flames. He managed a tired but affirmative nod. "I promise," he said, placing a hand on Jen's shoulder. She smiled weakly.

As the paramedics helped him into the ambulance, Edwin grew distant as he clutched the hard drive tight against his chest. At no point did he feel the black worm coiled around his ankle.

# The Blackout Killer

Rain pelts the window above the kitchen sink. Lightning reveals empty takeout containers near a stack of dirty dishes. The apartment went dark during a stretch of deep thunder, activating a continuous knock at the front door, a knock that sounds as if someone is unnaturally set upon confronting the inhabitant. That inhabitant—nervous, gray-haired Ager Bennett—sits by candlelight at his dining room table, browsing old newspaper clippings. *Another Child Slain During Power Outage, Murderer Dubbed 'Blackout Killer,'* and *Blackout Killer Escapes Asylum* are just a few of the headlines.

Ager, life-long bachelor and retired locksmith, refolds the clippings and sets them atop a book about phobias, anxieties, and sleep disorders; a book that assures him the knocks aren't real, that such things are triggered by his paranoia. Regardless, his nerves unravel; they are defenseless against blackouts. So he swallows another anti-anxiety pill—his third of the evening—and begins to jot down his thoughts in a spiral notebook (an often-used distraction while waiting for the calming effect of the medication).

*It was thirty years ago this very night,* the old man writes shakily, *same rundown suburb, same terrifying mix of thunderstorm and blackout.*

He pauses to consider the coincidence, then stares at his hands—hands that have done terrible things.

*I remember the night well,* he continues, *my coat dripping with rain as I climbed through the boy's bedroom window; my hand over his mouth—poor child!—as I woke him to the sight of my gargoyle mask; his reaction, like that of a stunned fish, as I breathed heavy and waved my* knife and whispered horrible things into his ear—demonic things, like "Behold the boogieman" and "Scream and I'll slit your throat!"

It was hellish, unforgivable! For the boy was different than the others—much too frail. He had no friends to speak of, no father figure, a drunken whore of a mother. At seven years old he was broken, unloved, uncared for. Yet, a desperate need to be free of my insufferable fear blinded me, led me to the despicable act of terrorizing innocent children. At the time I truly believed that each of my attacks dislodged a portion of that fear and placed it inside the victim.

Lightning cracks over the apartment. Dishes, utensils, and empty soda cans clink in the thunder. Tonight the blackout, the storm, what he perceives to be an escaped lunatic at the door, all this has fused into a singular anxiety that now asphyxiates his reality. And though his new, stronger medication will soon take effect, banishing the cruel knocks to silence, he cannot, presently, manage to stray from the dining room table; his legs are concrete pillars. So he returns to the writing:

I was a child myself when the fear entered me; when, at the age of seven, a dark, wispy ghoul crawled through my bedroom window and smothered me with its long hair and rank breath, waking me with sharp taps to the forehead—

Years later, a therapist would tell Ager the ghoul wasn't real, that it was simply a manifestation of his mother's murder—a murder carried out by his schizophrenic father—and that the traumatic experience had imprinted itself upon his frail being.

After whispering hideous things into my ear, he continues, which it did for no reason I've ever come to know, the creature straightened its gaunt black body and thrust out a large butcher knife. This it moved back and forth like a saw as it stared ahead with white, slit-like eyes. I screamed for mother, but she never came—I had all but forgotten she was dead. Then, without a sound, the creature bent its arms and legs, fell to the ground, and crawled out the window like a tarantula.

I shudder to think of it! Yet, this is surely what had led to my insatiable need to frighten children in a manner similar to the ghoul. Little did I realize, however, what I'd done to that one acutely sensitive child—

*that I'd planted a seed of discord deep within his soul, a growing evil that would plague every subsequent moment of his life. From then on the monster must have developed inside him like some grotesque larva, its toxins filling his bloodstream, poisoning his mind, altering the once innocent character of his soul, until at last the beast broke free and transformed him into a demented lunatic—the Blackout Killer!*

Sweat glistens on Ager's candlelit face, baggy eyes revealing a man in the throes of insomnia. With aching hand he continues to write:

*I followed the news closely and analyzed each of the killer's attacks, his patterns being so eerily similar to my own: the way he stalked his prey during storms and blackouts, the way he went about frightening children with a gargoyle mask. But my god, he killed most of them! Why? I didn't give him that. That was his own!*

Ager pauses to gather his thoughts. Suddenly the knocking, which had gone silent during the therapeutic writing, returns. At first it's like the quiet, steady drips of a faucet . . . and then the maddening *tap, tap, tap* of an awful finger against his forehead. Trembling, he clutches at his wiry hair and pleads with the door: "Stop! Just stop-stop-stop!"

But the knocking continues.

So he gets up, shuffles over to the kitchen sink, and peers out the window where lightening reveals wind-blown trees in bluish glow. There he lingers, hunched and silent, his palms pressed tight against his ears. He thinks of his mother's smiling face, her kind eyes watching over him. But angry children start to bombard his mind like thrown stones, nudging out the angelic presence of his mother. Soon his thoughts mutate, the children now dragging his frail body through a fiery cavern . . . . Meanwhile, the voice of anxiety whispers that the mix of storm and blackout will render his new medication ineffectual, and that the Blackout Killer has escaped the asylum to return the portion of fear he was forced to take thirty years ago.

A shrieking ghoul appears at the window and starts punching out the glass.

Wind roars into the kitchen, and Ager fumbles along the counter as dishes crash to the ground. He grabs the flickering candle from the dining room table and scampers to the front door, bawling like a child. There his heart pounds against his chest—*thump, thump, thump*—as the ghoul clambers herky-jerky through the window and drops to the floor. Breaths grow short as he fumbles with the locks. And then, in an instant, the storm softens and the knocking disappears; the medication has finally taken effect. "God, thank you," he mumbles, eyes glistening. "Thank you!"

But the medication has not dissolved the ghoul.

It now stands in the center of the living room, leaning forward at an awful, unnatural angle and wielding a large butcher knife. Ager drops his candle. Fire ignites the carpet and spreads to nearby furniture. Tears flood the lines of his cheeks. "Mother, help me, P-please, *help me!*"

And then, for the first time in thirty years, Ager sees them—sees beneath the long wet hair of the ghoul the sullen blue eyes of the little boy, the tortured soul who became the Blackout Killer. When the creature steps forward, the innocent, seven-year-old face becomes fully visible, superimposed over the misshapen head of the ghoul.

"It *is* you!" Ager sobs, falling to his knees. Flames rise and crack about him. "But what do you w-want with me? Why are you here?"

A knowing look from the boy, and Ager understands.

"No! I-I can't take it back, I just *can't!* I already have so much to bear! My victims . . . those *poor* men . . . childhoods ruined! It's all my fault, I know! Dear God, I know! I've suffered my whole life for it! *Please*, you mustn't——"

With a blank stare the creature jolts forward and grabs Ager by the head, pushing its drooling mouth against his left ear. Indistinct grunts and whispers pierce the old man's psyche before he is shoved to the floor. Falling to his side, he begins to cackle.

The ghoul, now a naked child, turns and runs back through the hissing flames and clambers out the kitchen window. Smoke fills Ager's grinning face as he loses consciousness.

Outside, the trees drip quietly; the storm has passed. The kitchen window stands intact and there is no sign of fire. Ager snaps awake. He listens: the door is silent. The medication has numbed his mind—he has no negative thoughts whatsoever, only an occasional spurt of cackling. With glazed eyes he reaches for the still-burning candle, struggles to his feet, and wobbles up to the couch for support.

And then—*could it be?* Someone is knocking at the door again. Ager pats down his hair, straightens his posture. "Yes? Who's there?"

No answer.

He cackles involuntarily, throws a palm over his mouth.

*It's just the maintenance man, here to explain the power outage,* whispers one of his old therapists. *Yeah, that's who,* the self-help book proclaims. *See, there's nothing to worry about, you old fool,* confirms the soothing voice of the medication.

Candle in hand, Ager walks over and puts an eye to the peephole. The hallway is pitch black; not a single emergency light or human outline to be seen. A woman whispers his name—a voice not heard since childhood.

"Mother, is that you?" He puts an ear to the door.

In a rush of excitement he unlocks the bolts and pulls off the chains. He twists the steel knob, steps back, lets the door swing wide open. A wall of darkness greets him. He raises the candle, filling the hallway with weak, amber light. There, dozens of children stare back at him. Dozens of children wearing gargoyle masks.

# Making Amends

He is making amends to his victims
in a swarm of their ghosts, enduring
the blades, beatings, wringing hands—
each angry shade tearing at his soul
as their own deaths rebloom and blacken.

For thirty years, few women walked
that city alone. In dreams they shrank
beneath his police sketch, took to prayer
in the gore of his wake. The law's eyes
went bloodshot seeking answers.

When at last he died in old age, a pack
of shades broke from limbo, scurried
like bats to the gates of hell. There they
howled and wept and dragged him away.
He is making amends to his victims.

# Spiral of Flies

Asher took a long, hard look at the pair of stilts resting against the wall of his living room, a hypnotic Deftones song echoing through his wavering consciousness: "I watched you change, into a fly . . . ." In a sudden rage he threw his beer bottle at the MP3 player, took up a nearby axe, and chopped the stilts into a thousand pieces.

He awoke on the couch a few hours later, disoriented and hung over. All was quiet but for the crackling radiator and the hum of the refrigerator. If it hadn't been for a hint of sunrise pressed against the east window, and a faint glow from beneath the bathroom door, he'd have been in complete darkness.

Mumbling to himself about having smoked some bad shit, Asher looked up and noticed that the walls of his apartment were now exceedingly high and made of amber. Flies zipped back and forth between them, bumping into one another and spiraling down in aerial combat. With a crackling of air, a tall, looming figure on a pair of stilts shimmered into view beside the TV, its body black save for two red orbs on an otherwise blank face. A long flat object lay stretched across its upturned arms, while a small mandrill squatted sleepy-eyed on its left shoulder.

With a sudden huff from its scarlet nose, the monkey stretched a clawed hand toward the object and nudged it forward; there it split apart and wafted down to the floor like a pair of feathers. Asher rubbed his eyes, unsure of how to respond. Wasn't this all just a hallucination? A waking dream? With a yawn he nonchalantly reached down and dragged the objects to his lap for closer inspection. There they gave the impression of oversized insect wings, like those of a house fly. The moment he realized this, they disappeared.

"What the hell?" He looked to his visitors for an answer, but the elongated figure and its monkey were gone. Just then the apartment reverted back to its original state, a blazing sunrise now pouring in through the open window.

Asher lit a cigarette and contemplated all he had just seen. Explanations rose and fell away. A few satisfactory ones stuck, and in time, his nerves began to settle. After all, it wasn't his first time hallucinating.

By noon he was back at his old routine, sprawled out on the couch with a can of beer between his legs. A group of scantily clad women stood around yelling at each other on the TV; annoyed, Asher shut it off. In that moment he heard, or thought he heard, a moan coming from inside the bathroom. Just the neighbors, he thought to himself. But then the silent, bizarre creature and its servant monkey came to mind.

"So much for drowning nightmares in alcohol," he grumbled, taking a long drag from his cigarette. That's when he looked down at the faded track marks on his arm; and that's when the cause of his hallucinations became clear: smack.

Smack. Horse. Heroin. H. Many names for the same monster. Asher had recently been using, but managed to quit before the urges got too strong. A residual amount, he figured, or mild withdrawal coupled with the intake of alcohol and marijuana, must have triggered those visions. What logic he still possessed encouraged him to sober up, to give the drug ample time to leave his system. But that hideous figure had raised his anxiety to new heights, so he grabbed another beer and rolled a joint.

The remaining afternoon was spent listening to music and strumming his guitar. He was beyond all worry, beyond the constant image of his brain spiraling down a toilet with piss and shit. Gone, too, were thoughts of that haunting figure and its ambiguous agenda.

But it wasn't long before the weed had transformed him into a heap of tangled nerves. "Man, I need *balance*," he said to himself, pacing the apartment and punching at his head. "Fuck—I need some H!"

Pausing to remind himself of the progress made regarding heavy drugs, of the promises made not only to himself, but to his mother and sister, Asher lay down and tried to sleep off the cravings.

To no avail.

By evening he began to shake with fever. That's when the stilts reappeared at the wall, their quiet, inanimate presence enticing him over. Soon a buzzy, inner voice went plugging through the silt of his brain: *Go higher, Asher. Go higher.* Ridiculously, he covered his ears. The mantra only rose in pitch. He pressed his palms tight against his head and hummed, but the voice breached all barriers. And then, through trembling hands, he began to hear that Deftones song from the previous night, the lyrics revealing something about a man changing into a fly . . . .

A new thought sparked in Asher's mind, one that made him stand straight up: *destroy the stilts!* That's when the axe reappeared on the coffee table and he made good use of it. That's how another night passed without H.

But he awoke to more hallucinations in the pre-dawn of the next morning. Once again the walls turned to amber and took on abnormal dimensions. Flies zipped around in circles beneath the ceiling, buzzing with laughter, and the dark figure on the stilts reappeared with its monkey and fly wings. But none of it disappeared like it had the previous morning; instead, the room retained its nightmarish qualities and the figure merely backed into the shadows, leaving behind the wings. Something turned on the bathroom light, door now ajar, and the moaning inside grew more audible.

Asher sank into the couch with a fresh joint and turned on the TV—an attempt to ignore the lingering hallucinations. The day carried on as usual, and then it was night. To his horror, the visions perpetuated; in fact, they had grown more vivid, more ominous.

In the end they broke him.

"Just one bag," Asher pleaded over the phone. "No-no—two."

Cowering in the amber light beneath the laughing flies, Asher sat at the edge of his couch and wept.

*   *   *

The first dose expelled the hallucinations right away—an expected result, and Asher began to relax. But soon the stilts reappeared, this time walking themselves back and forth in front of the TV. The axe appeared next, again on the coffee table. So he injected a second dose into his swollen arm, and then a third, and a fourth. The objects remained. By then he no longer cared, and this time, instead of chopping the stilts into pieces, he climbed into them. He wasn't sure how he did this, but he did. He climbed into them, and the walls and ceiling expanded to accommodate his new height.

For a time he ambled around in the stilts, somehow possessing a natural ability. Indescribable sensations blasted through his body and instilled a cliché oneness with the universe. A loud buzz arose from behind, and when he glanced back he saw them: large, beautifully patterned insect wings rising off his shoulders.

Magazines began to flutter and dust took to air. Thousands of flies appeared all around him: some alive, others trapped inside the colossal amber walls. The stilts grew and lifted him higher. The wings accelerated, and he felt ready to fly. But then the moaning from the bathroom reached his greatly attuned ears, and in glancing down he noticed that the door was now wide open—a long, spiral stream of flies going in.

From that point on, Asher could somehow see *inside* the bathroom. It was as if his sight had been usurped by a telescopic lens. And through that perspective he saw himself lying motionless in the bathtub—a syringe stuck in his arm, his naked, skeletal body heavy with purple veins that throbbed in the fluorescent light. Hundreds of flies stood on the rims of the sink and bathtub, rubbing their front legs together in anticipation.

Asher shut his eyes to escape the vision, but the mandrill suddenly appeared on his shoulder and he lost his balance, the stilts cracking apart and falling into the darkness. And when the man in the bathtub let out a sick, sludgy moan and puked on his own chest, Asher joined the spiral of flies and laughed as he zipped around the convulsing body—laughed and laughed like it was the funniest thing he had ever seen.

# The Dark Island

Thane arrived at the Wisconsin Indian Reservation around noon, having just bounced along ten miles of dirt road plagued with pot holes and tree limbs. Lake Michigan, sunlit blue and specked with gulls, sat low in the east behind an autumnal stretch of maple and birch. His pickup came to a skid at the general store and launched a dust cloud at a waiting tribal officer. The officer, whose black hair hung past his shoulders, lifted an eyebrow and watched the cloud pass through his legs.

Thane dropped from the truck and tore off his sunglasses. "Sheriff Stalking Bear?"

"Ike," the man said, gripping Thane's hand. "You must be Mr. Swink, from the Field Museum. Nice to meet you."

"Nice to meet you, too. Call me Thane."

The pickup coughed and pissed some fluid, then fell silent. Thane withheld eye contact just long enough to suppress his embarrassment.

"Might wanna get that checked out." The sheriff's tone had a laugh pushed up against it.

Thane slid the sunglasses into the v of his flannel shirt, then turned for a quick look around, taking note of the post office, a hardware store, and a single-pump gas station. A one-room schoolhouse, its playground overrun with children, sat near the lake. He also noticed a diner, small marina, a few clunker cars, and a scattering of ranch-style and prefab houses. Though most of the dwellings were nestled along the tree line, a few driveways could be seen shooting off into the woods.

"Nice town," Thane said. "And the fall color is spectacular."

"We do our best," Ike replied, glancing about casually. "So Thane, tell me more about why you're here today."

"Well," Thane began, "like I was saying on the phone the other day, I came across this old file at the museum which mentions a research cabin on one of your islands. Said it was built in 1894, for a botanical expedition. You mentioned having seen it yourself."

The officer nodded.

"Now, what I suspect is that maybe, just maybe, it still contains a few plant specimens, maybe even a data book or journal—items of great interest to our botanical department."

"You anticipate finding plants collected over a *hundred* years ago?" Ike asked. "I take it they were somehow preserved?"

"Definitely. Plants can last hundreds of years if pressed and dried properly, so long as they're kept in a safe environment. My guess is that the botanists kept a steel herbarium cabinet there. Those things are rust proof, insect proof, even fire proof. And they're airtight. According to my research, the surviving botanist didn't take anything back with him but his dead comrade."

"The man the museum claims was murdered by the shaman guide."

"Yes," Thane said, "but honestly, I don't know much about that, and I certainly don't take any sides." He shrugged. "I just assume things went south right from the get-go. Clash of cultures or something.

Ike nodded. "Wouldn't be the first time."

"Anyway, I hope the tribal council doesn't take issue with me being here, seeing as I work for the museum. That *was* a long time ago."

"Certainly was. And no worries, Thane—you're quite welcome here. We understand you've a job to do."

Thane gestured to the store. "If you don't mind, I'd like to go in and grab some packing tape for the boxes."

"Boxes?"

"Yeah, cardboard boxes. For hauling back the plant specimens."

"Ah, I see."

Thane followed Ike into the store. A spritely old man, eating what appeared to be a blueberry muffin, smiled at them as they passed.

"Afternoon, Jaime," Ike said to the young woman behind the cash register.

"*Bozho!*" she replied. On the counter to her left, displayed with candy bars, cheap toys, and fishing tackle, was a stack of locally baked goods containing "healberries."

"What's healberry?" Thane asked the sheriff.

"Oh, just a local name for blueberries."

The men entered a nearby aisle where Thane grabbed a granola bar.

"Healberries grow on the island," Ike went on, "in areas where it's darkest. Which reminds me: the canopy is very dense over there. I hope you brought a flashlight."

"Certainly did," Thane said.

They turned down the next aisle, where Ike paused. "Oh, by the way, there's something I need to mention before you head out there today."

"Sure, go ahead."

"Now, the tribal council doesn't contest that the cabin is museum property, so do with it as you please. That said, if you're at all tempted to explore the island, even to collect specimens, then please, come and see me first. You're a scientist, I'm sure you understand about permits, safety, all that—political mumbo jumbo. Anyway, it's my responsibility to mention it. So keep that in mind, and try to wrap things up as quickly as you can." His hands were tucked into his pockets, thumbs out. "Get back by six and I'll treat you to the best fish n' chips you ever had."

"I just might take you up on that," Thane said. "And in regards to collecting, the only plants I'm interested in are those old flattened ones in the herbarium cabinet."

The sheriff gestured to a messy arrangement of office supplies. "Tape's over there."

Thane approached the shelf, his finger hovering over each item until he found the tape. He grabbed two rolls and turned to Ike. "Ready if you are," he said.

Whispers floated up from the checkout counter, where a woman holding hands with a doe-eyed little girl stood talking with Jaime. The women grew silent as the men approached.

"*Bozho!*" Thane said, smiling as he placed his items on the counter. The women smiled back, and the little girl, who nibbled on a blue-tinted muffin, regarded him with a countenance he thought seemed a bit wise for her age.

"Four or five hours, tops," Thane said as they reached the dock. Sunlit gravel crunched beneath their boots, and each man carried a few items from Thane's truck. "I work fast, and I'm not easily distracted." He paused, then added, "I know I don't look it, but . . . but I'm actually a quarter Native myself, on my mother's side. In fact, just coming here . . . well, I was kind of hoping to get in touch with my heritage a bit. If that's even possible in such a short visit."

Ike walked up to a canoe and turned to Thane, smiling warmly. "I'm sure you will, kid. And I can tell you've got Native blood—it's in your mannerisms."

Thane studied the man's face, unsure if he were joking or not.

"Better get going," Ike went on, squinting at the horizon. "Rain's coming."

Thane only saw clear afternoon sky.

"Be careful now," the sheriff continued. "And remember, those woods are dark, even on sunny days, and the terrain is uneven. No trails, either." He regarded the botanist, sort of father-like. "You look fit. What are you, twenty-five 140?"

Thane let out a quick laugh. "Nope, thirty-five 150. Just like you, right?"

That made the sheriff's eyebrows jump, and he actually laughed. "Kid, try older than dirt and none-of-your business!"

\* \* \*

The shoreline of the island was a composite of sand, pebbles, and ragged juts of limestone. Thane rowed until his oars scrapped bottom, then hopped out of the canoe and dragged it ashore. After retrieving his gear, he grabbed the stack of flattened boxes and attached them to his backpack with carabiners and bungee cords. A nearby sign marked the direction of the cabin, and there he tried, in vain, to take a GPS reading of his location; unsuccessful, he presumed, due to the rainclouds that had suddenly appeared overhead, turning the lake pallid gray.

Raindrops smacked the sand as he stepped into the woods. Taking out his flashlight, he soon discovered why the woods were so intrinsically dark: as far as he could tell, the canopy was a nearly solid, interwoven mass of tree limbs and thick vines. It seemed to form a roof, albeit a leaky one, for some ecological purpose he had yet to discern.

Random drops from a steady rain began to penetrate the canopy and fall through the darkness. Thane turned from side to side as he advanced, investigating the ecosystem through the long beam of his flashlight. Spidery ferns, squat shrubs, and other shade-tolerant flora not uncommon to the Great Lakes region surrounded him. The soil, he observed, was moist and sandy, and the air was humid. Ghostly orchids appeared often, as did pockets of strange phosphorescent fungi that seemed to fade like moribund stars whenever he approached them.

Though botanical curiosity often kept his thoughts on the island's floral diversity, Thane occasionally daydreamed about his Native ancestors. How would these woods have been navigated a hundred years ago? he wondered, scrutinizing his surroundings. And although he was well aware that most Native Americans no longer acted in this manner, such thoughts still gave Thane a sense of pride in the small but ever-rising presence of his Native heritage.

The rain let up after nearly half a mile, and the canopy thinned out just enough to put away the flashlight. A tall, rounded boulder appeared ahead of him, and, walking up to it, Thane pushed his palm into its springy layer of moss. A cloud of spores rose into the air, and Thane had to turn on his heel to avoid being hit in the face by the yellow dust. In doing so he noticed, just beyond a stand of pines, what appeared to be a small cabin. Thane forgot about the spores and made a beeline for the structure, his equipment clanking as he pushed his way through the ferns.

Of basic design, the cabin was otherwise striking in its mottled aspect, the roof and sides made colorful by a patchwork of bluish lichen and crimson vines spread over chestnut-colored wood. Half a dozen bur oaks formed a tight circle about it, their long, gnarled limbs climbing the log walls while smaller branches punched through the cracks.

With a wobbly turn of the handle, Thane pushed the door inward, then stepped aside as a downpour of rust flecks fell from the hinges. Fungous air blew against his face and lingered on his skin for what seemed an exploratory moment before a bright orange spider plopped onto the leaf litter and scuttled toward him. To his surprise, he had to kick at it several times before it finally went the other way.

Mice scurried off as Thane stooped through the doorway with his flashlight. Inside, the log walls appeared to be solid but for an area or two of rot, while overhead a few precarious rafters held up the low ceiling. A hard slab of earth composed the floor, and along the bases of each wall grew that strange phosphorescent fungi Thane had seen earlier, and which, as before, seemed to shut off their intrinsic light at the moment his eyes caught sight of them.

There were two cots: one against the north wall, another against the west (the shaman, Thane conjectured, must have slept outside). Along the east wall stretched a wooden table and a pair of rickety chairs. Candles, degraded books, and an array of scientific instruments were strewn about the table, covered in lonely decades of cobwebs, pollen, and tiny growths. A curious oak limb corkscrewed through the lower right corner of a four-paned window, reaching across the table like an eldritch arm. Other panes were cracked and dirty, and a few shelves, crooked but tightly packed with crumbling books, hung above the work table at either end. Shoved beneath the table was a short herbarium cabinet.

Thane sighed with relief. "Wow, it's actually here! Look at that old thing!"

Unable to contain his excitement, Thane quickly untied his equipment, hung an electric lantern on the unsightly oak limb, and dropped to his knees before the metal cabinet. There he paused, quiet and reverent, as if the box was the long forgotten idol of some woodland god, and he, the chosen one, was led here to receive its untold secrets. Suddenly he became nervous. Had the botanists followed protocol in keeping their specimens preserved? Would he see the standard: flattened plant clippings tucked within sheets of newspaper? Collection numbers written on the newspaper margins, those numbers corresponding to data inside a notebook he was sure to find inside the cabinet? These things he dared hope as the handle was turned and the steel door creaked open.

The damn thing was empty.

"Christ, are you kidding me?" Thane hit the table top with a fist.

Grasping the edge of the table for support, Thane shot his flashlight into the depths of each narrow shelf. All that remained was a thin scattering of plant debris—proof, at least, that the specimens had been there. But where were they now? And wasn't there a journal or data book somewhere?

Thane shut his eyes against the red of encroaching anger. A groan swelled in his throat. How could he return empty-handed? How could he face his superiors after persuading them to fund this little excursion? And then it occurred to him that in his haste, he had not checked the backs of the last few shelves. So he bent down low and scanned again. To his surprise, a leather-bound notebook sat at the back of the bottom shelf.

Thane rejoiced as he pulled the notebook out into the light. He opened it carefully, so as to not crack the yellowed pages, and skimmed its numerous entries. Most were written by Andrew Wilhelm, the botanist who had survived the shaman's attack.

Thane tugged at his sparse beard. "*Now* we're talkin'."

An entry at the back of the notebook caught his attention: *August 21, 1894: What the shaman has taught us about the regional flora is of great value, and will prove beneficial, if not profitable, to the civilized world. But there is much he refuses to tell us, and such stubbornness does not sit well with Dr. McKiness. I now fear for the safety of our shaman guide.*

Thane flipped ahead. In an obvious hurried hand, the last page of the journal (August 22nd) went on to say, *Let this entry be a record of events, for something unholy has taken the life of my colleague, Dr. Timothy McKiness, and at present I do not know if I will be allowed to leave the island alive.*

*It all began the prior afternoon, when McKiness mercilessly kicked the shaman as he sat outside meditating (McKiness never did have much tolerance for the man's heathen ways). As the old Indian writhed in pain, a terrifying echo suddenly shot through the woods, a noise I can only describe as an amalgam of animal sounds—of hissing snakes, chattering crows, and various grunts and growls, all seeming to come from the four cardinal directions. At this point I lost all nerve and promptly took refuge inside the cabin. From there I watched helplessly as an assortment of contorted shapes emerged from the woods and swarmed about McKiness, the man himself spinning in a circle and shouting "Damn you all!" with his cross held high. It was all to no avail. In an instant those awful shapes merged into a ghostly black noose and snatched McKiness off the ground with an awful crack. The shaman then floated off into the woods, and I never saw him again.*

*At that moment I must have been struck with fear or insanity, for I calmly took to my cot, closed my eyes, and fell into a long, deep sleep. This morning I woke to a horrible sight: McKiness sprawled out in a corner, his eyes blankly staring, his body covered in wet leaves and glowing fungi.*

"Whoa! Wilhelm *was* crazy," Thane remarked. "No wonder they had locked him up in an asylum!" He glanced uncomfortably at one of the cots, then took a deep breath and eased his shoulders. Those people, he reminded himself, were long dead. Furthermore, the documents at the museum indicated that there was uncertainty about what had actually transpired between the three men. Maybe Wilhelm's account had been concocted in an effort to admonish the botanists of any wrongdoing in what might have been perceived as a murderous act against the shaman. Or perhaps the shaman had killed McKiness in self-defense, only to be killed by Wilhelm. But even if Wilhelm's story had been accepted, then why confine him to an asylum? The whole thing smelled of a cover-up.

But Thane pondered such questions only briefly, realizing the truth was now lost to history.

He shook off his concerns and returned to the journal: *August 15, 1894: Collection #158; medium-sized shrub discovered in ravine just NW of cabin; plant 1.2 meters tall; leaves deeply serrated; scraggly branches covered in dark blue fruit. Genus undetermined; possible relative of our native blueberry.*

Most interesting, however, were the following comments: *A very infrequent shrub, thus far seen nowhere else in the region but on this island. The shaman is very secretive of it, revealing only that his ancestors have deemed it void of medicinal value. McKiness and I have feelings to the contrary, for the savage disapproved strongly of our collecting samples. He claims, rather unconvincingly, that it is sacred to his tribe.*

With those words, Thane decided he would visit the aforementioned ravine and search for a descendant of the mystery shrub, curious to know if it truly had any taxonomic relationship with common blueberry (or "healberry," as it was referred to locally). He recalled the sheriff's warning against collecting, so in lieu of a fresh specimen, he decided to only take photographs.

A few minutes later, while adjusting his field gear outside the cabin, Thane noticed a large boar staring at him from roughly ten yards away. "Hey there, bud," he said, surprised. "How'd *you* get so far north, huh? Hitchhike?" As Thane pondered the unexpected presence of the animal, which was hundreds of miles outside its natural range, it stepped back into the gloomy woods and disappeared.

\*     \*     \*

To his surprise, the shrub—or most likely a descendant of the shrub—still persisted where the men had originally reported it. A robust specimen, its branches were heavy with clusters of dark blue berries. Thane plucked one and turned it over in his palm beneath the beam of his flashlight. The berry was soft, thinly-skinned. He pinched it and put his nose to the excreted juice. The smell was potent, citrusy. He knew well the flora of the Great Lakes region, but this one stumped him. Hybrid blueberry? New species? Determined to find out, Thane pulled a sandwich from his pack, sat on a nearby log, and spent the next hour documenting the shrub with notes and photographs. Lastly, out of habit, he clipped a small branch and shoved it into his backpack.

Moments later a boar, perhaps the same one from earlier, appeared from behind a large maple just a few yards downslope. Closer this time, it seemed almost sentient, as if pondering the man's presence. When Thane went for his camera, the animal disappeared.

Back at the cabin, Thane tossed the plant clipping onto the work table and lit a few candles. He cracked open the journal and read another entry: *The shaman has, on several occasions, boiled and eaten the shrub's berries. And though it appears to us that his vitality greatly increases after ingesting the fruits, McKiness and I have chosen not to sample them until thorough testing can be done. After all, it is well-documented that Indian tolerance of certain foods is greater than that of the white man. Nonetheless, we have high hopes that the plant contains medicinal properties of which we are presently ignorant, despite the shaman's insistence that it does not.*

That was the last thing Thane remembered reading.

The candles were burning low when a series of leaf crunching footsteps jarred Thane awake. Dizzy, he checked his watch and peered out the window, startled to see moonlight.

A sudden *bang* hit the cabin like a giant fist, dislodging dirt from the walls and ceiling.

Thane jumped to his feet and stumbled back, then leaned forward and grabbed the edge of the table for support. Vertigo overwhelmed him. With mouth agape he listened as the footsteps made their way to the front door. There they stopped. Utter silence followed. Without warning, the door blasted inward and crashed to the ground. Thane fumbled along the table for his knife and grabbed it.

A dark, snorting cloud retreated from the doorway—a pair of tusks left stuck in the fallen door.

"Hey! HEEEEY!" Thane yelled, his words stretched out like a retreating flock of birds. He stumbled back in the flickering candlelight, head full of jolting synapses. His hands, now trembling, flew to his face; the knife fell to the ground and stuck into the dirt. Yanking his hands away, he noticed that some of his fingertips were stained blue. "Damn it, I'm hallucinating!" Thane wiped his mouth with his shirt. "Residue from those berries must've gotten on my sandwich—shit!"

The sound of tribal drums arose in the distance; the footsteps returned.

Thane crouched to retrieve the knife as the last candle burned to its end. In that same moment, a rush of adrenaline kicked away his vertigo. He ran outside with his flashlight and wavered through the night's patchwork of shadows and moonbeams.

"Show yourself!" Thane demanded.

A nebulous figure appeared in a nearby mass of ferns.

Thane jabbed his knife at the shape. "You! If you think this little prank is going to scare me off then you're sorely mistaken! Sheriff Stalking Bear gave me special permission to be here!" He shot out the flashlight, but there was no one in the beam. The drumming vibrated the earth beneath his feet. He turned; the figure now stood in a slant of moonlight just a few yards away—an old Native man, sunken-faced and naked but for a bone necklace and the head garment of a boar. He arced forward and swayed his arms like a storm-blown willow, releasing an amalgam of sounds neither distinctly human nor animal. The sounds melded strangely into words, snapping at Thane so suddenly he tripped and fell backward over an emergent root.

"BURN THE BOOK!"

Shadows crept in from the four cardinal directions—some along the ground, others through the trees. With frenzied blurs the old man began to shape-shift in rhythm to the drums: the lanky body cracked, stretched, and expanded; the boar hide trembled and slid back like a slug, disappearing into a thick, hovering fog at the crown of the man's head; hoary fur sprouted along face and quivering limbs as a pair of tusks grew forth from an enlarged mouth; full moons flashed in the eyes as he landed on all fours and charged, extended hands morphing into hooves.

Thane curled himself into a tight ball and covered his head. The drums burrowed into his psyche, calling out to him like the mother of some orphaned animal. He expected death, but the grunting, spitting beast took a final sharp turn and crashed through the woods behind him.

Thane sprang up and ran back into the cabin. There he lifted the fallen door and propped it into place with the herbarium cabinet.

"Burn the book? What *book*?" Thane said to himself, pacing the tight confines of the cabin. All the books around him seemed on the brink of dust. Had he meant the botanist's journal?

Not chancing to find out what the old man might do next, Thane gathered his gear, packed away the journal, and raced back through the woods to his boat. When he finally broke free of the claustrophobic darkness and stumbled onto the moonlit beach, he was relieved to find that his canoe was still there. He rowed to the mainland in what might have been record time, then pulled the boat ashore and collapsed onto the sand.

*   *   *

Thane woke to the sound of snapping twigs. He sat up in a daze, his head foggy.

"Come get warm," said a familiar voice. It was Ike, sitting on a log and tossing twigs into a crackling fire.

Thane shivered, his clarity returning in short bursts.

"Find what you were looking for?" Ike asked, as if nothing were out of the ordinary. He took up a pocket knife and a long stick.

"The plant specimens were gone," Thane said flatly, spitting sand off his tongue. "Taken, I suspect, so I wouldn't learn about the healberry, or whatever else grows out there." He glared at Ike. "And I was chased off by a crazy person. But you knew that already, didn't you?"

Ike shrugged his shoulders.

"I mean, why not just tell me the cabin was empty in the first place? Why bother having me come all this way?"

Ike examined his stick, decided it was good.

"But you guys didn't know about the journal, did you?" Thane went on. The item in question lay next to the fire, most of its pages ripped out. Thane pointed at it. "Why, Ike? What's so special about that island? And the healberry bush?"

The sheriff began to carve a sharp point into the end of his stick. "Let's just say I've been kicking around for quite awhile. 'Older than dirt,' remember?" He chuckled lightly. "But you've got to boil the berries first, otherwise—"

"They're a hallucinogenic," Thane interrupted. "Yeah, I'm quite aware of that. And they're extremely potent—I barely ingested any. Which leads me to wonder about the plant's overall potential. You know, like its medicinal properties. I mean, it could—" Thane paused to think it over. "Never mind, I get it. If a pharmaceutical company ever got wind of it they'd be all over this place. Things would get complicated."

Ike put aside his sharpened stick and picked up a second one. He glanced at the journal, then scrutinized Thane's face. "Yep, you found it all right," he said. "Or maybe it found you."

"Huh?"

Ike nodded at the journal.

"But you're destroying it," Thane accused.

"I guess you don't remember. It was you, Thane. *You* built this fire. *You* burned those pages. That is, before you passed out."

Nearly a minute of silence went by.

"Hmm, that old man," Thane began pensively, "and the boar . . . that was my subconscious mind coming out symbolically through hallucinations. Is that right? And my

90

suppressed ancestral roots, they were trying to reveal themselves the whole time."

"Jeez!" laughed Ike. "That's a bit wild. Don't think too hard on it, Thane. Not everything needs to boil down to logic. Just know you took your first step on a new path; the one you were seeking."

Ike finished carving the second stick. "Sounds like the old man gave you quite a show. Don't judge him too harshly, though. After all, he's very protective of the island, of the nourishment that keeps us all so healthy. And keep in mind that scare tactics are a common device in a shaman's bag of tricks. He did what he felt was necessary. But let me tell you something. He did *not* kill McKiness. That was the island. One day you'll understand."

"Wait, back up. What are you saying? That the crazy old man back there is the *original* shaman? Like, 1890 guy?" Thane snorted. "C'mon man, he'd be long dead by now."

Ike reached down between his legs, picked up a jar of healberry jam and held it up.

"Oh yeah," Thane said. "You guys are older than dirt. Sure, got it."

He turned to look out across the starlit waves of the lake, shaking his head doubtfully even as he began to accept the things he now knew to be true, or at least let himself believe were true. A screech-owl called nearby; its trill, mingled with crickets and lapping waves, helped lull Thane out of his frustration.

"So what happens now?" he asked.

Ike reached down and shoved his hand into a small plastic bag. He offered Thane a sharpened stick.

"Marshmallows."

"What?"

"Graham crackers, marshmallows, a dab of healberry jam. My own version of s'mores. Quite good. Care for one?"

Thane got to his knees and looked down the length of the shore. Colored leaves floated down from the rustling trees, landing on the beach. He scooted forward, grabbed the journal, and tore out the remaining pages, tossing them into the fire. He stared into the rising flames as the beat of a distant drum filled his ears.

"Gimme that stick," he said finally, a glint of humor in his eye. "And that, too."

Ike winked at him, and passed the jar of jam.

# PUBLICATION HISTORY

. . . . . . . . . . . . . . . . . . . . . . . . . . . . . . . . . . . . . . .

These stories and poems were originally published as follows:

"Belch," *Space and Time Magazine*, 2012
"The Blackout Killer," *Tales to Terrify* (audio podcast), 2016
"Charon Falls into the Styx," *Bards and Sages Quarterly*, 2012
"The Dark Island," *Electric Spec*, 2015 (as "Potawatomi Island")
"Deal Down at the Hospital," *Liquid Imagination*, 2012
"Faerystruck Down," *Tales of the Talisman*, 2013
"Ghoul of the Enamel," *Spectral Realms*, 2015
"The Girl with the Crooked Spine," *Electric Spec*, 2014
"The Hunchback's Captive," *The Horror Zine*, 2014
"Intimate Universes," *Tales of the Talisman*, 2014
"Making Amends," *Star\*Line*, 2013
"Misery of He Who is Outside the Realm of Man," *Tales of the Talisman*, 2013
"Not for Mortal Eyes," *Disturbed Digest*, 2014
"Penumbra," *Black Petals*, 2011
"The Politician's New Heart," *The Speculative Edge*, 2012
"Post-Funeral Mission to Mars," *Tales of the Talisman*, 2014
"Red Icicles," *Flashes in the Dark*, 2011
"Sketch by Sketch," *Rose Red Review*, 2014
"Spiral of Flies," *Morpheus Tales*, 2013
"Strings," *New Myths*, 2012
"Time to Grow Up Where There's No Time at All," *Mythic Delirium*, 2012
"The Tramp Clown's Secret," *Space and Time Magazine*, 2014

"The Unfortunate Heartbreak of Faritook the Earwig," *State of Imagination*, 2011

"What We Know of Goddesses," *Tales of the Talisman*, 2015 (as "We Call Them the Gods")

# ACKNOWLEDGMENTS

Thank you to my wife Kelly Sturner for her support, her feedback on the material in this book, and for believing it was worth publishing. Thank you to Martin Andersson for proofreading. Thank you to Amelia Royce Leonards for the use of her wonderful artwork. Thank you to John C. Mannone, S.T. Joshi, and David Lee Summers for their generous comments on the book. And thank you to everyone that has supported my writing over the years; it is very much appreciated! Lastly, thank you to my son Garion, who helped me reunite with my childhood imagination. Such an invaluable gift!

# ABOUT THE AUTHOR

Jay Sturner is a writer, poet, and naturalist from the Chicago suburbs. His writing has appeared in *Space and Time Magazine*, *Spectral Realms*, *Tales of the Talisman*, and many other publications. He has been nominated twice for the Rhysling Award, and in 2019 one of his poems was featured on a segment of NPR's *All Things Considered*. In addition to writing, Jay is also a professional bird walk leader. His website is www.jasonsturner.blogspot.com

# ABOUT THE COVER ARTIST

Amelia Royce Leonards is a graduate of Montserrat College of Art in Beverly, where she spent four years baffling her peers and professors with drawings of goddesses and antlered women. Her work is influenced by the beauty of ancient myth, folklore, and the natural world around us. She can usually be found somewhere deep in the woods, sketching odd creatures and eating chocolate chips. You can find more of her artwork at www.etsy.com/shop/Ameluria

Made in the USA
Lexington, KY
23 November 2019

57545355R00063